ASHLEY BEEGAN

You'll See

To those who have lost themselves in the dark,
may you find your way back to the light.

Contents

Prologue

The room they put me in was too white. It was so bright it made my eyes burn. The walls, the sheets, and the lights all blended into one endless void of blinding emptiness. It felt like a punishment, even though they all kept promising it wasn't.

I curled tighter into myself on the hard mattress and pulled the thin blanket up to my chin. The material was cold and scratchy against my skin. Someone had cracked the door open just enough for the faint voices in the corridor to seep in. They were the voices of the doctors, I think. Or maybe it was my parents.

The thought of my parents made my stomach twist. They were the last people I wanted to see. I wasn't sure why. Everything in my brain felt blurry, like someone had scrambled my memories and left me with only the frayed edges. But I knew I wanted to be far away from my mother.

I reached for my wrist and ran my thumb over the fresh bandages that wrapped tightly around the brand new cuts. The cuts destroyed the mini bear tattoo. I'd only had it done a month ago, much to my mothers dismay.

The cuts on my wrist no longer hurt despite being so fresh. Even the ever present pain in my heart was distant. Whatever drugs they'd pumped into my system back at the other hospital had dulled it. But the shame was still sharp.

I hadn't wanted to die. Not really. It was the nightmares that made me do it. I'd dreamt again of fire and the boy and I couldn't take it anymore. He was everywhere.

Even then his blank stare bored into me from the corner of the room. I squeezed my eyes shut and tried to make him go away. It was silly, really. Closing my eyes never helped. When they were shut the memories came back, so I saw him anyway.

In my memories, hot flames roared vividly around me and suffocated my every breath. The same white-eyed boy stood just beyond the fire with his small shoulders hunched. I reached for him and called out. He didn't move. He never did in my dreams.

I ripped my eyes open as the door creaked open wider and a figure stepped into the room. It was a nurse with a clipboard tucked under her arm. The nurses here dressed funny. They wore T-shirts and jeans rather than the uniforms they wore in the other hospital. She was a lot older than me with soft features and a kind smile. Though it didn't reach her tired eyes.

"Piper Roberts? Hi, I'm Dixie," she said. Her voice was gentle enough, but she sounded detached somehow or far away. Or maybe that was the drugs, too. "How are you feeling?"

My eyes flickered up to hers. I didn't respond. My throat felt too dry, and I didn't have an answer, anyway. What was I supposed to say? I can taste smoke from a fire that was only in my head? Or there was a silent boy with a blurred face watching us both that she couldn't see? I glanced at him. He was staring at her rather than me, and he did not look happy.

How could she not see him? Or at least feel his anger? I'd

never get to go home if I told her the truth about what I could see. Though no doubt my mother had bared all of my secrets to the staff there already. If my mother thought I was crazy, then the mental hospital certainly would too.

But Dixie was undeterred by my silence. She stepped closer to my bed, pulled a chair up, and sat down. She never took her eyes off me.

"Your parents are here," she said slowly. "They're waiting to see you but only if you feel up to it."

I swallowed hard as my chest tightened. The last thing I wanted was to see either of them. I didn't want to see the disappointment on their faces, or that fear in my mother's eyes. And the boy really hated it when Dad was around. Especially if I tried to talk to him when the boy was here. I couldn't even help him with the shopping list last week. The boy did not like him at all.

"I don't want to see them." My voice cracked, barely audible even to my own ears.

"That's okay." Dixie nodded and jotted something down on her clipboard.

I wondered what she'd written about me on there. Probably something like: *Absolutely nuts. Must stay locked up forever.*

"We'll let them know," she continued. "I understand you're a little unsure of your dad at the moment."

"He's not my dad," I snapped before I could help myself.

"Yes, yes." She nods. "I know you're worried he is an impersonator. We can keep him away, Piper. Don't you worry about a thing."

I wanted to ask her why I was there. Why did they bring me to this place that smelled like bleach and antiseptic? A place where the walls were too white and the voices too distant and the boy was not happy. But deep down I already knew the answer. I was broken. They wanted to fix me. That will never happen.

He wouldn't allow it.

"Piper," Dixie said, her tone shifting slightly. "You mentioned a boy before to your mother from your dreams. Do you want to talk about him?"

My stomach dropped.

"No," I said quickly, the word tumbling out before I could stop it.

I can't believe she just said that in front of him. I glanced over to the corner. He was still there with his face still turned towards the nurse. He didn't like her. She was making him furious.

"That's okay." She studied me. Her pen hovered over her clipboard. "But sometimes it helps to talk about these things to make sense of them."

"We don't need to talk about him," I whispered. I shook my head and gripped the blanket tighter.

The boy's head snapped around to look at me. My stomach flipped. His eyes were blank but I could feel his anger as if it were my own.

Then it started. The faint, rhythmic tapping I hated so much. It only usually happened around dad. The boy's index finger drummed against his leg, the sound was too sharp and loud for something so soft. Like tapping a pen off a table.

Tap. Tap. Tap.

My heart twisted. He only tapped when he got really mad. I glanced at Dixie, but she was too busy making another note to realise what was happening. She couldn't hear the tapping.

The sound crawled under my skin and grew louder and louder until it drowned out everything else. When I looked back to meet his white eyes, his lips curled upward into something that could have been a smile or a warning.

"Okay." Dixie hesitated, then finally looked up at me and nodded again.

The tapping stopped. My gaze darted to the corner. It was empty now. He was gone. I swallowed hard in relief and looked back at Dixie.

The boy was standing right behind her.

"We'll talk more later. For now, just rest."

She stood and moved toward the door. My breath caught in my throat as I watched her walk past him. He stared up at her the whole time she walked away. She stopped at the doorway.

"You're safe here, Piper. We'll take care of you."

Safe. I almost scoffed. The word felt hollow and meaningless. How could I be safe when the demons were inside my brain? No one else could even see them, never mind fight them. There was no getting away from them either here or at home. I'd rather be lying in bed with every bone broken over my brain being so broken.

As the door clicked shut behind her, the boy's head snapped back to stare at me. His expression softened. He was happy she'd gone.

I closed my eyes and let the memories of fire come again. The boy stood there as usual in the flames. He was just out of reach. I didn't know who he was or why he haunted me. But deep down, I knew one thing. That boy was real. I just needed proof.

Swanson

etective Inspector Alex Swanson woke to the quiet of a dark, January morning. He turned over and instinctively reached out toward Summer to rest his palm on the curve of her growing belly. Her brown hair spilled over the pillow in a way which framed her face, and her skin felt warm against his palm.

He left his hand there until he felt a tiny foot press against his palm and he was satisfied that they were both okay, then pressed a gentle kiss to her forehead and pulled himself out of bed. Summer didn't stir. She never did lately. This pregnancy was taking a serious toll on her energy levels.

He tiptoed down the hall to the bathroom. The cool air of the room greeted him as he turned on the shower. He checked his beard in the mirror to ensure it didn't need a trim. His broad-shouldered frame made the bathroom feel smaller than it was. It reminded him of the cosy proportions of his old Ockbrook cottage.

He'd left the cottage to move into the house Aunt Barb had left for him in her will, much to the dismay of her two sons. They'd refused to speak to him since finding out they hadn't inherited the house. So as far as Swanson was concerned, it was a win for all involved.

The four bed detached property was enormous compared to the cottage so it had been the right move. They'd never have fit four people comfortably in it or in Summer's old flat.

The water wasn't as warm as he liked and the old pipes had rubbish water pressure, but it still cleared the sleepy fog in his head. As he stepped out onto the shower mat, the sound of clattering in the kitchen pulled his attention downstairs. He listened intently for a moment. Joshua was awake.

He stepped into the hallway, the wooden floors creaking slightly underfoot. The house still carried faint traces of Aunt Barb. The faint scent of lavender clung to the hallway from an old reed diffuser she'd left behind. There was her old floral wallpaper in the downstairs loo and the antique mirror in the hallway. But Summer had begun to make it theirs. A framed sonogram sat on the hallway table next to Joshua's latest school photo.

He quickly got dressed to check out the noise. Eight-year-old Joshua was already awake and out of bed. He was at the kitchen counter pouring his own cereal. He was Summer's double. His dark, curly hair stuck up in wild directions, and his pale blue pyjamas were slightly too short at the ankles, a sign of yet another growth spurt. Swanson leaned against the doorframe to watch the scene unfold with a small smile.

"Careful there, mate," he chuckled. He crossed his arms as Joshua gave the cereal box a little too much tilt.

"I'm fine doing it myself," Joshua said. "It's only cereal."

"I can see that." Swanson pushed himself off the doorframe and walked over as Joshua grabbed the milk and tipped it over the bowl. "But you might want to dial back the milk a bit, yeah? Or you'll have soup instead of cereal."

Swanson turned as Summer appeared in the doorway. She

was freshly showered and dressed smartly in a pale green trouser suit. She'd pulled her dark hair back into a ponytail.

"Morning." She smiled at the sight of them as she entered the kitchen. "I hope you've made me a bowl of cereal too!"

"Yes. I made you breakfast!" Joshua announced and puffed out his chest proudly. He held up the bowl with both hands, offering it as proof.

"Did you now? That was very kind. Thank you." Summer replied, arching an eyebrow at the spilled cereal left on the side.

She kissed the top of his head and took the bowl. Joshua set about making another for himself as she sat down at the table.

"After you've eaten, you need to get dressed super quick for school. We're running a little late," she said. "My fault. I'm just so tired all the time lately."

"I'll head in when you leave for school and see you at work after you've dropped him off," Swanson said as he glanced at the clock.

"You will," Summer replied. "Are things still quiet your end?"

"I'm not going to say yes to that because I will jinx it, but I will nod," Swanson replied.

"That's still a yes," Joshua piped up. He furrowed his brow as he glanced up at Swanson.

"No, it's a nod. It's different."

"So, if anything crazy gets reported today it won't be his fault." Summer smiled.

"Exactly."

Joshua still looked unsure, but they ate together before he ran off to get dressed, returning five minutes later in his grey school trousers and crested red jumper.

"Are you all ready?" Summer asked.

"I suppose so." Joshua nodded.

He grabbed his backpack and pulled it over his small shoulders. Swanson opened the door for them, standing in the cold air outside as Summer and Joshua climbed into her car.

"Have a good day both of you. Love you." He leaned down to the window.

"Love you too," Summer replied. She blew him a kiss before driving off with Joshua waving from the back seat.

A faint unease tugged at his stomach as he stood by the door and watched Summer's car pull away. He pushed it down and climbed into his beloved BMW. The drive from their new home in the pretty village of Darley Abbey to the police station was only five minutes long. Which was much quicker than the commute from Ockbrook. It was one positive thing about moving, even if he missed the cottage dearly.

Though the drive through the centre in rush hour traffic was still frustratingly slow at times. It ended up taking him almost twenty minutes to reach the car park at the rear of the station. Detective Inspector Rebecca Hart was already waiting at the entrance for him. She leaned against the doorframe with her arms crossed against a puffy winter coat. It was so thick for her slight frame it bordered on ridiculous.

"You're late," she snapped once he was out of the car.

"It's not even nine o'clock. I'm early," Swanson replied with a smile. "Anyway, I'm a juggling family man now. Stop moaning at me."

"Someone's got to keep you in line," Hart shot back as she pushed off the door and fell into step beside him. "Let's get this morning meeting with the ice queen over with, yeah?"

"You mean the love of your life?" Swanson scoffed. "Don't let her hear you call her that."

"Why not?" Hart replied.

"I can't imagine she'd be happy with that as a nickname."

"Yeah, well. You should hear what I call her in bed."

"Jeez, Hart. Stop!" Swanson held up a hand. "I don't need to know what you two get up outside of work, thanks!"

"Well, I have to hear about you and Summer!"

"What do you mean? I never tell you anything like that about Summer."

"Women talk, Swanson." She winked.

"Not in that level of detail I hope!"

"You have no idea what women are like when we're alone." Hart laughed as they reached the briefing room.

He might be sick of hearing about her sex life, but it was nice to see the old Hart coming back slowly after the trauma of last year.

The station was the same red-bricked beast it had always been. It was two enormous floors of terrible coffee, flickering strip lights, and the faint scent of burnt toast from the break rooms. The heating system worked only when it felt like it, and the air always carried a lingering trace of damp files and sweat. Swanson had spent half his career here, and there had been times it felt more like home than the cottage.

As they stepped into the briefing room, the chatter among the team died down. A board at the front displayed a series of photos. They were blurry CCTV stills along with a missing person's report.

"Everyone, settle down," yelled Detective Chief Inspector Jane Murray. Her eyes flicked to Hart, but she glanced away. She cleared her throat and tapped her pen against the table. "We've got a few things to cover today, but let's start with this. This woman's name is Hayley Smith, and she was last seen one week ago leaving work to go home. She didn't appear for her shift the next day and no one has seen her since."

She gestured toward the board. He instantly regretted his nod to Summer at the breakfast table. His gaze fixed on the grainy image of a woman's face on the screen. Something about her eyes made his chest tighten. She had the same brown hair and eyes as Summer, and she looked wary, like she'd been expecting the worst. Hart nudged him hard with her elbow.

"Told you yesterday we wouldn't stay quiet for long."

Piper

I t was always the little things that got to me after someone died. Like hearing their weird sneeze in your head or their particular way of running down the stairs. Or the way my front door looked so wrong without their shoes next to mine. After my parents were murdered, it didn't truly hit me until a couple of days before Christmas when no card arrived written in Mum's tightly woven handwriting. That was months after they died.

For Evelyn Beeley, it was being able to roll my eyes when she called me on a Saturday to cover another shift. I'd have loved to hear her beg me to come into the psych ward one more time.

"Please, Piper. Sara's sick and Ian put shit all over the walls again."

I stifled a giggle at the memory by covering it with a cough. Laughing during a funeral would not be a good look. Especially not when so many people here are already suspicious of me. They already watched me too closely, as if waiting for a slip-up.

It was my first time in a church since my parents' joint funeral three years ago. Though that funeral wasn't in this church. It was nearer to their home in the quaint east midlands city of Derby. This church was much darker, and it was currently filled with soft whispers and the muted rustling of clothes. It was much busier too. Only eleven people turned up to say goodbye to my parents, including the priest.

A woman two rows in front of me in an enormous hat turned to whisper something to her blonde friend, who turned and flashed me a steely look. I've always felt like I stick out too much. I was too tall and too pale. My hair wasn't quite brown or blonde but something in between, and its waves framed a snobby face that drew attention whether I wanted it to or not.

That day was no different. I felt their eyes on me. Not for my looks, but for the suspicion that hung over me like a cloud. They saw me acting distant and assumed I was hard-hearted. What they didn't see was the way my hands trembled at my sides or that my heart raced every time someone glanced in my direction.

I wrapped one hand around my wrist and thumbed the ripped flesh there that would never heal. The scars had ruined the little bear tattoo, giving him marks he was never meant to have. But I loved his marks. It made him damaged, just like me.

Some people find their bodily scars embarrassing. I hid mine for the funeral in a long-sleeved wrap dress that fell to my knees, but only to prevent questions and stares. I find comfort in the ugly marks. It was a physical sign I'd been through worse times and I came out the other side.

Sunlight filtered through the stained glass windows to cast fractured colours onto the coffin at the front of the room. The scent of incense was so strong I wasn't sure it would ever leave my nostrils. I couldn't wait to breathe fresh air again.

I let go of my wrist and twisted the fabric of my black dress that fell around my knees. I couldn't stop fidgeting. My hands just needed something to do.

I didn't cry like the people around me, despite being sad. I've never been a crier. I'm more likely to curl up and put a film on when I'm sad rather than cry. Or stuff my face. Though now I'm on a strict pre-pregnancy diet, I can't even do that.

Someone near the front sobbed quietly. It blended with the low, steady voice of the priest. I could barely hear him. His words floated by as if they weren't meant for me. I fixed my eyes on the coffin and tried to look normal.

Adam Bell stood beside me. His large hand rested gently on my back. I loved looking at Adam. He was too tall and too pale just like me. I loved the way his kind, dark eyes softened the sharp angles of his jawline and the way his lean frame made him seem effortlessly elegant. Sometimes, I could barely take my eyes off him. I was too tall for most men, but Adam made me feel small.

He'd also been so patient with me since it all happened. He'd been trying so hard to take care of me. It was one of the plus points of dating an experienced therapist. And I appreciated it, I really did, but no matter how much he tried I could not shake this emptiness inside me. There were no tears and no gut-wrenching sadness. I only experienced a numbness that felt like it was hollowing me out from the inside.

"Are you doing okay?" Adam leaned in, his voice soft and close to my ear.

I nodded, though I wasn't okay. I wasn't anything.

"Yeah. I'm fine," I whispered.

The words were automatic by now. *Fine.* That's what people wanted to hear.

Except for experienced therapists.

"We'll talk when we get outside," he whispered, giving my hip a squeeze.

He always seemed to know what I was feeling. I glanced

toward Evelyn's husband at the front. I wondered if he always knew what Evelyn was thinking. They'd been together way longer than Adam and I.

We weren't close, but I'd met him a few times when he came into the hospital to pick Evelyn up if her car was in the garage. He was a big guy who spent a lot of time in the gym. That's where he'd met Evelyn. Usually, he was smiling and cracking jokes to whoever was around to listen.

But there were no jokes from him that day. He hunched his shoulders, and his grief was raw. You could feel it even from a distance. I should've felt something similar. Evelyn had been more than just my boss. I'd known her for years. She'd given me my first actual break after I finished studying psychology at twenty-two years old. She trusted me when I didn't trust myself.

The psych ward was not a peaceful place to work. So we'd had drinks together after finishing long shifts and talked about life. She was one of the few people who didn't judge me for my scars. She was the closest thing I had to a friend.

So why didn't I feel more? Why wasn't I falling apart like everyone else? Adam's hand pressed a little firmer into my back, reminding me he was there.

"If you need to step out, just say the word," he murmured.

"No. I need to stay." I shook my head.

I needed to be there, even if it felt wrong because of my lack of emotion. Not out of respect or grief. I hated funerals as a mark of respect. Crowding into a church that none of us would ever usually visit was no way to honour the dead in my opinion. I didn't understand that logic at all. But leaving would make me look weak or guilty, and I'd had enough of people looking at me strangely already.

The priest continued. Though his voice barely registered as he spoke about Evelyn's life, her kindness, and her dedication to her work that he knew nothing about. I didn't really listen. All I could think about was the last time I saw her alive and the way she'd smiled at me as we got into the car.

How everything had changed so fast with the flash of a masked face and the crack of a gunshot.

I blinked, forcing the memory away. My fists clenched, but the service finally ended and the noise of people moving brought me back to the present. The crowd began shuffling toward the exit as they trailed behind the casket murmuring softly to one another.

When it was our turn to leave the pew, Adam clasped my hand and guided me toward the door. He kept close like he was afraid I might crumble at any moment. I didn't. I couldn't. Not yet. Not in front of people, even if it was only him.

An icy breeze hit my face as we reached the steps outside, and I let out a slow breath, relieved it was over. Only family members were going to follow the casket to the gravesite, which was fine by me. The chatter of people around me sounded distant like I was hearing them through a layer of thick fog.

"You've been really strong," Adam whispered. His deep voice was full of warmth. "I'm proud of you."

I nodded but his words felt hollow. I didn't feel strong; I felt empty. The fact that I was still standing wasn't a sign of strength. It was pure survival. Guilt is heavier than grief, and that's what I was carrying. Guilt that someone as worthless as me was still alive, and that someone beautiful like Evelyn wasn't.

And extra guilt that someone had murdered her in the same way as my parents three years ago. It made it all feel like it was my fault somehow. When I saw the gun being pointed through the car window, I thought for sure it was for me. I still wonder if they got the wrong person. What if I was their intended target? It left me with nothing but questions with no answers in sight.

The police questioned me after her murder. I was the only one there after all. But the only thing in common with my parents' shooting and Evelyn's was me. And Michael Grey had already confessed to killing my parents straight after the event. The police arrested and charged him then closed the case. It had nothing to do with him or my family. So why couldn't I shake the feeling of guilt?

Even after the police released me I felt like it was all connected somehow. Adam's arm tightened around me and pulled me a little closer as we approached the car.

"Let's get you home," he said, his voice soft. It was his soothing therapist voice. I usually loved it, but at that moment it caused a fleeting irritation. "You've had enough for today."

I wanted to tell him that getting home wouldn't change anything. I'd still feel like this. But I nodded. It was easier to let him think he could help.

We got into the car and I stared out the window as Adam started the engine. I watched as the other mourners slowly dispersed either to follow the casket or head to the bar across the road for drinks. My mind wandered back to Evelyn. I remembered her laughter and sharp wit and her no-nonsense attitude at work. The way she covered her mouth when she laughed or the way her forehead creased when she was angry. It all seemed so far away now. Like she was someone I'd read about in a book, not someone I actually knew. Adam glanced at me.

"Do you want to talk about it yet?" he asked gently.

"Not right now." I shook my head.

He nodded, and we drove in silence. I glanced back at the window. I wondered if the dead were really at rest or if they'd somehow come back for me. Like the little boy who used to visit me.

The car slowed at a red light. I glanced out the window, my breath fogging the glass. I saw someone standing by the edge of the churchyard. A small figure half-hidden in the shadows of the trees. My stomach tightened.

It was probably nothing. Just a mourner who'd stayed behind. But my chest ached with unease, and I couldn't shake the thought of Evelyn. Of her smile before we got into the car, or of the masked face that came from nowhere. Or how the smell of burnt gunpowder filled my nose for days.

"Piper?" Adam's voice pulled me back. His eyes flicked to me, soft with concern. "You okay?"

"Yeah. I'm fine." I nodded quickly.

But I wasn't fine. My hands trembled, and I pressed them into my lap to stop them. As the light turned green and Adam drove again, I glanced back at the churchyard. The figure was gone.

Piper

A week after Evelyn's funeral, I stood in the kitchen taping thick bubble wrap around the barely used porcelain plates that were rimmed with pretty blue flowers. I stared out of the window of my Victorian flat as I wrapped the last plate. They were the same plates my mother bought me when the psychiatrist released me from the hospital. I'd moved straight into my own place at nineteen years old, and made sure it was far away from home for a fresh start.

I'd googled the best place to live in England and came up with Harrogate, which had won the title of being the happiest place to live in the UK three years running back then. That was nine years ago, though it felt like no time at all had passed some days.

Harrogate was a spa town with beautiful, historic buildings. I'd been so excited to start my new life. Where could be better than the happiest place in the UK? It was the heart of Yorkshire and seemed perfect. It was supposed to be a place where nothing could go wrong. I couldn't think of anywhere nicer to live. Never did I think I'd see someone get shot in Harrogate.

It was just after noon when my phone rang. Its sharp tone sliced through the quiet of the old flat. I stared at the name on the screen: Pinevale House. My heart skipped. It was the call

I'd been half hoping for and half dreading. It was the same one that would help me change my life and force me to move away from Harrogate if I made the leap.

"Hello?" I answered.

"Hi, Piper, this is Sue Blake from Pinevale House," said a raspy voice whose owner had smoked far too many cigarettes. "I'm just calling to say you did great in the interview. We'd love to offer you the position of mental health support worker. Congratulations!"

There it was. The words I had been waiting for. The same words that meant I could move back home to the pretty city of Derby. I should've felt relief and excitement. Maybe even a little satisfaction at finally getting away from everything that had happened with Evelyn and the nasty whispers from her loved ones, but none of those feelings came.

Instead, a tight knot formed in my chest. As much as I needed the job, it was more than just a new role. It was a whole new life, and that meant moving to the one place I had been avoiding for almost ten years. My parents' house.

"That's great," I said, forcing the words out. "Thank you."

My stomach twisted. I didn't move, barely even blinked, as Sue kept talking. It was happening. I was really going to move.

"We'll send over the paperwork this afternoon," Sue continued. Her voice was far too bright for my mood. "The team's really looking forward to having you on board. We can't do the training this week, but we can do it the following week. So we'll see you next Monday, yeah?"

"Yeah, sure. Next Monday. Thanks again," I replied, barely registering what she said.

I hung up and stared at my pale reflection in the kitchen window. Pinevale House was a non-secure mental health home and far quieter than the secure psychiatric hospital I was used to. That was for male criminals who had committed serious crimes like murder, rape and sexual abuse. They were all diagnosed with serious personality disorders like antisocial or schizotypal personality disorder.

Pinevale House was more of an open home for rehabilitated or less dangerous patients. The job would be easy after dealing with everything that happened at the secure hospital on a daily basis. It was what I wanted. What I needed, even.

Plus, moving back to Derby would be another fresh start seeing as Harrogate hadn't quite worked out. But my parents' house was frozen in time since their untimely deaths, and the thought of cleaning it out finally was making it hard to breathe. I ran a hand through my dark hair and called Adam. He picked up after a few rings, sounding distracted.

"Hey, how are you doing?" he asked.

"I got the job at Pinevale," I replied as I sat down at the table. There was a heavy pause before he responded.

"Yeah? That's great."

His tone didn't quite match his words, and he fell quiet again. I didn't speak either as the silence stretched out in front of us. We both knew what it meant. I was moving away from him.

We'd previously chatted about the fact I'd be two hours away if I moved, and I had left it up to him whether he wanted to make the offer to move with me. Though I knew deep down there was no way he'd leave his patients. He wasn't mad about me choosing to move further away—he'd thought it would be good for me—but he *was* sad. That was worse. I swallowed away the lump forming in my throat.

"That's such a good thing for you, babe," he said eventually.

"Yeah," I replied, though my voice lacked conviction just

like his.

I waited for him to say more, but the silence stretched between us again.

"Piper, you're not going to do it. Are you?" he finally said. "You're not going to move into that house? You don't have to. You could rent somewhere else in Derby. Maybe somewhere near Pinevale House. There's no rush."

His concern tugged at something inside me. I knew he meant well, but moving into my parents' house wasn't something I could avoid forever. It wasn't just about the job at Pinevale or saving money, though that would certainly help with the credit card debt I'd racked up since my parents' death.

This move was about not running from my past anymore. It was about creating happy memories for once, but also about figuring out my forgotten ones at long last. I needed to remember what happened to me as a child. It was time to stop being scared.

"I can't afford to rent," I said. My throat tightened. I knew he'd say that. I had never told Adam about my credit card debt. "The job is much less pay wise. I'll have to sell it eventually, and I can't do that if I don't clear it out."

"It's just there are a lot of memories there. I don't want you going back and ending up... you know."

"I know." I tried to keep my voice steady but I could hear the tremor in it. "But I'm not eighteen anymore. I can handle it better now. Plus, I have you to talk to."

"I know." He sighed. "I just worry about you being there alone, especially after everything you've been through recently. That's a lot for anyone to take and now you're moving back to a place that's haunted you."

"I'll be fine, Adam. It's just a house."

"It's not just a house. It's where you had a—"

"I know," I cut him off, not wanting to hear him say the word breakdown.

I couldn't go there again. It had taken months to see Dad as just Dad and to push the boy out of my head. But sometimes I still caught glimpses of him. Just a flicker around a corner or a flash of white eyes. They were gone when I blinked, but it was a reminder that he might return. And I never wanted that. Adam shifted gears, his voice softening.

"Look, if you really want to do this, I'll support you. I'll come visit as much as I can. Maybe I can even look for a job over there so I can be closer to you."

"You'd do that?"

I hadn't expected him to say that so soon. We'd only been together for a year after all. Not to mention he had his patients to think about. We'd been through a lot together in that year though. Mainly my fault.

And although he didn't really know it, there was a possibility I was pregnant with his child. I hadn't told him I was ovulating when we last had sex. I didn't want to put pressure on him. But I had everything crossed that this was the month it would happen. We both needed a bit of light in our lives.

"Of course," he said. "You're not doing this alone, and I think it's time for us to take the next step, maybe. If you want to."

The relief I should've felt earlier finally trickled in. Maybe I could do this. With Adam by my side maybe it wouldn't be so bad.

"Thanks," I whispered. "I'd love that. I love you."

"I love you too."

We talked a bit more about logistics, such as when I'd move

and when he could visit, and by the time we hung up I felt marginally better. But the nagging thought of having to be in that house and the memories that came with it loomed in the back of my mind like a dark cloud.

I spent the rest of the afternoon packing up what I could. I got the easy bits done and dusted. It was mostly clothes and a few boxes of things I might need for the next few weeks. I couldn't fit too much into my parents' house because it was still full of their stuff, and I owned little anyway. Mainly thanks to having racked up twenty grand's worth of debt across three credit cards in three years.

The credit cards had gone on nothing, really. I spent it on takeaways and nights out with Evelyn and weekends away with Adam. I used it to deal with life because I couldn't function any other way. Spending was a way to forget about the lost memories that haunted me.

But not anymore. I planned to face life head on for once. Adam and I both knew that moving back to my parents was going to help me remember my forgotten past and once I remembered it, I could deal with it. There'd be no more spending then. I was stronger with him by my side.

Plus the thought of cluttering my parents' house with remnants of my Harrogate life felt wrong, like I'd be intruding on a space that no longer belonged to me. Even though I'd spent my later childhood there, it never truly felt like home.

I tried not to dwell on that part of my life too much. Not that there was much to dwell on. I could only recall the last eight years of childhood, anyway. I remembered nothing from below the age of ten. There was a blank space where my childhood should have been. No birthdays, no Christmas mornings, no scraped knees or bedtime stories. Just nothing.

I glanced around the kitchen at the bubble-wrapped plates and half-packed boxes which suddenly felt like they belonged to someone else. The knot in my stomach tightened. Moving back to Derby was supposed to be the start of dealing with my issues. But I couldn't shake the feeling that I wasn't just about to walk into a house full of memories. I was walking straight into a storm.

Then the doorbell rang.

I flinched, my pulse kicking up. I wasn't expecting anyone. Wiping my hands on my jeans, I walked to the door and pulled it open.

"You're still here?" Adam stood on the step, hands in his pockets. He forced a smile, but something in his eyes was off. There was sadness there. I felt it too. "I thought you might need a cuddle."

I smiled as I sank into his warm chest, but the truth was I needed something much bigger than a cuddle. I just wish I knew what.

Swanson

Swanson leaned against the counter of the police station's compact kitchen nursing a glass of water. He watched Hart fiddle with the temperamental coffee machine. He'd known her long enough to offer no help. It wouldn't go down well if he did.

Summer sat at the small table in the kitchen with her hands wrapped protectively around her stomach. She did that more often now that her bump was getting bigger.

"Bloody thing," Hart muttered. She jabbed at the machine as it gurgled half-heartedly.

"You break it every time you touch it." Swanson smirked behind his beard.

"It breaks when I touch it because it's old enough to be in a museum," Hart shot back, her sharp grin returning as she finally coaxed a splash of coffee into her cup.

"You're the one sleeping with the boss. Get us a new one."

"Budget cuts," Hart replied smoothly, leaning back against the counter with her steaming cup. "Blame the higher-ups for making us drink this swill."

"Now you even sound like her. You could be healthier and stick with water like me."

He tipped his glass towards her while she rolled her eyes.

Summer looked up from her phone with a small smile.

"If you two are done arguing over coffee, do you actually want to solve this case?"

Hart raised an eyebrow but said nothing and took a long sip of her coffee instead. Swanson glanced at Summer.

"We're heading to Ilkeston this morning," he said, setting his empty glass down. "Hayley Smith's workplace is not too far from your mum's place. Oakleigh House."

"That's the mental health home, right?" Summer frowned. "Is that where her manager reported her missing from when she didn't turn up for her shift?"

"That's the one," Hart chimed in. "The manager, Linda Reeve, called it in after Hayley didn't show up six days ago. She reported it the same day. Apparently, she's the type to live and breathe her job so they knew something was off straight away when she didn't turn up. They passed it over to us since they can't find any leads as to where she might be and nothing has been taken from her flat. We'll need to do a press release soon."

"No family or close friends to visit?" Summer asked.

"None that we know of." Swanson shook his head. "Linda Reeve said Hayley kept to herself and she lived alone. No one's seen or heard from her since the day before Linda reported her missing. That was when she clocked out of work."

"So, no personal connections and a high-pressure, low-paid job." Summer's brow furrowed. "That doesn't exactly scream work-life balance. You think it's possibly a suicide?"

"That's what we're going to figure out," Swanson said, glancing at his watch. "Come on, Hart. Time to hit the road."

"Fine. Let's go." Hart sighed dramatically, cradling her coffee cup like it was a lifeline.

Against his better judgment, he let Hart drive them for once in her old MINI Cooper. He folded his long legs awkwardly into the cramped passenger seat and silently prayed for survival.

He needn't have worried. Thanks to the evening rush hour traffic the drive to the old mining town of Ilkeston was slow. But after almost an hour, Oakleigh House loomed ahead of them.

It was a squat, nondescript building with peeling paint and a faded sign that proclaimed it a friendly safe haven for mental health recovery. Swanson glanced at Hart as they exited the car. The place looked anything but friendly.

At the front desk, a red-haired receptionist glanced up through thick glasses as Swanson and Hart approached. She looked barely out of her teens. Her oversized blue polo shirt was emblazoned with the Oakleigh House logo. Her bored expression didn't waver as she plastered on a wide, obviously fake smile.

"Can I help you?" she asked.

Swanson pulled out his badge. "DI Alex Swanson, Derbyshire Police. This is my colleague, DI Rebecca Hart. We're here about Hayley Smith."

"Have you found her?" The receptionist's eyes widened.

"Not yet," Hart said. "We need to speak with your manager about her disappearance, please."

"Give me a sec." The receptionist nodded, reaching for the phone. "I'll let her know you're here."

Swanson let his gaze wander around the room as they waited. It wasn't very homely for a safe haven. They'd painted the walls a dull beige, and the potent smell of disinfectant hung in the air mixed with fish and chips.

After a few minutes, a stout, middle-aged woman with

shoulder length, bottle blonde hair emerged from the back office. She wore the same blue polo shirt as the receptionist, except she had a name badge pinned neatly to it that read Linda Reeve, Manager. Deep lines framed her tired eyes, and she greeted them with a strained smile.

"Detectives," she said, her voice brisk but polite. "I'm Linda Reeve, the manager. Nice to meet you. I heard you're here about Hayley. I'm glad your lot are finally taking this seriously. Please come into my office and take a seat."

Swanson stepped into Linda's office with Hart close behind. The space was modest and dominated by a desk with chairs arranged on either side. A pin board on one wall included lots of photos of patients taken in the home. Swanson glanced at it briefly and noticed quite a lot of them featured Hayley Smith. She had a wide smile with no sense of the dread he'd spotted in her eyes on the CCTV stills. Swanson sank into a chair, Hart took the seat beside him and Linda settled opposite.

"We're trying to piece together who she is and her movements before she went missing," he began. "What can you tell us about her?"

"Hayley was one of our most dedicated staff members." Linda folded her arms with a sigh. Her expression clouded. "She's been with us for over three years. Lived for the job, really. She never talked about family or friends other than the odd mention of a boyfriend called Tom. I got the impression she was lonely. But she had a way with the clients that live here. They loved her. She always seemed to know what they needed."

"When did you last see her?" Hart asked, pulling out her notebook.

"One week ago," Linda said. "Last Monday. I did tell your

officers this already. She clocked out at the end of her shift and said she'd see us the next day at seven a.m. but she didn't show up. I tried calling her, but it went straight to voicemail. She'd listed Tom as her next of kin. But the phone number we have for him is out of service. That's when I called the police."

"Did she ever mention feeling unsafe? Any issues with patients or colleagues?" Swanson asked.

"She mentioned nothing to me." Linda hesitated, her lips pressing into a thin line. "Hayley cared deeply about her work and was always worried about doing something wrong even though she was a star employee. If a patient was bothering her, I'm sure she would've told me."

Swanson nodded.

"We'd like to look around if that's okay? It would be good to speak to a few of her colleagues. Maybe some of the clients that worked with her."

"I'm afraid that's not possible." Linda stiffened, her polite facade hardening. "Our clients are classed as vulnerable adults, and we can't allow police officers to interact with them without an official responsible adult present. You'll need the appropriate permissions."

Hart bristled beside him but Swanson spoke quickly before she could put her foot in it.

"It wouldn't be official police interviews, more of a simple chat, but understood. We'll get the paperwork sorted. Is there anything else you can tell us about Hayley?"

"Not really. Like I said, she spoke little about her life outside of work. She acted totally normal that day."

"Would you say she ever appeared depressed?" asked Hart.

"Just lonely maybe, like I mentioned already. She was always quite chatty, especially when speaking about Tom, but now I look back and wonder if she made him up. His number doesn't work, and she dodged questions about him quite a lot. Like where he worked or where he lived. I thought she just didn't want to share too much about him. But if she did lie about him, then what else was she hiding?"

"Hmm. Well, we'll get the permissions sorted to chat to the patients and be in touch shortly. Please let us know if anything else comes to mind."

After they'd said their goodbyes and stepped outside, they made their way back to Hart's precariously parked car. A man loitering nearby caught Swanson's eye. He was tall and gaunt and his clothes hung loosely on his thin frame. He looked up, and his dark, unblinking eyes fixed on them.

"You see him?" Swanson asked, nodding toward the man.

Hart followed his gaze.

"Yeah. Looks like he's been waiting for us."

They approached cautiously. The man didn't move. His posture was rigid and his expression unreadable.

"Can we help you?" Swanson asked, his tone firm.

The man reached into his pocket. Swanson stiffened, but all the man produced was a folded piece of paper. He extended it toward them without a word.

Swanson took the paper and unfolded it carefully. His frown deepened as he read the shaky handwriting scrawled across it. There were two words written on it. Perry Vance.

"Who's this?" Swanson asked, looking up. But the man had already turned and was walking away, his steps hurried and uneven.

"Hey!" Hart called after him, but he didn't stop. He disappeared around the corner.

"I guess we've got a new lead to follow up." Swanson stared

down at the paper.

"Yeah," Hart said, her voice tight with suspicion. "But why do I feel like this one's going to be a pain in the arse?"

"Because it probably is." He glanced back toward the corner where the man had disappeared.

"This place doesn't feel right," he muttered.

"What tipped you off?" Hart rolled her eyes. She glanced at him, her eyebrow arched. "The manager stonewalling us or the creepy man?"

"Both." Swanson folded the paper carefully and slipped it into his pocket. "Let's get back to the station. We've got some digging to do."

"Maybe Summer can help with the vulnerable adult thing," Hart muttered as they walked back to the car.

Her words made the case settle heavier on his shoulders. After what happened last year, the last thing he wanted was Summer caught in the middle of another case. Especially one that already felt rotten

Piper

Later that week, I set out on the two-hour drive to the familiar bustle of Derby. I took the long way there to appreciate the views, and so I had longer to change my mind.

The roads gradually narrowed, and Harrogate's elegant buildings gave way to winding lanes and sprawling fields. As I approached the Peak District route, the landscape changed entirely from the city. Tall hills rose around me draped in mist, and the rolling green seemed endless. I always found it both beautiful and strangely isolating. It had been years since I'd taken this route, since their funeral, and with every passing mile my decision settled heavier on my shoulders.

I pushed the gloomy feeling away and continued into the city of Derby, the place I grew up in from the age of ten. My memories before then were all but gone up in smoke with the fire, our old home, and the rest of our belongings. My first memory is of those flames. I remembered the heat of the flames, and a thud to the head. I never was sure about what happened exactly. Mum said I'd fallen down the stairs while running from the fire and bumped my head.

I think a part of me never wanted to remember my life before the fire. Maybe there was a reason I'd forgotten. But with my mental health spiralling out of control again, along with my credit card balance, I knew I needed to get a better grip on my life. And that started with remembering my childhood. Even if I remember something awful, something ten-year-old me *wanted* to forget, it would fix the gaping hole I've felt ever since those flames tore my life apart.

I drove straight through the city and out past the other end to reach Darley Abbey. Darley Abbey was a former historic mill village which was a short walk from the River Derwent, and the prettiest place near the city in my dad's opinion. The river cut smoothly through the landscape, its dark waters moving lazily past the old mills and carrying the echoes of Derby's industrial past.

The village's old cottages, narrow winding lanes, and sprawling green spaces made it feel like a step back in time. It was far removed from the rush of Derby's streets. But reality settled in as I turned onto Cleaver Close. My parents' house came into view, a four-bedroom red-brick detached sitting at the end of a long, uneven driveway.

It looked the same as it had the day I left. The shutters I'd paid to be installed on the windows after their deaths were closed, and ivy crawled up the brick wall above the red front door. Someone had even trimmed the lawn neatly just like every other lawn on the street.

How the hell had that happened?

Confused, I looked around as if I would see a culprit walking away with a lawn mower. The street was empty of course. No lawn mowers in sight.

The knot of unease in my stomach pulled tighter. Someone actually had the nerve to set foot on the property without permission and mow the lawn. Who would do that?

I parked the car on the road outside and gripped the steering wheel as I tried to gather the strength to step out. I closed my eyes and sucked in deep breaths as a psychiatrist had taught me to do a long time ago.

I'm not sure how long I sat there, but eventually I was calm enough to leave the car. The keys felt heavy in my hand as I climbed out and made my way up the path that sat between two patches of the neatly trimmed grass. My feet crunched on the gravel, the sound unnaturally loud in the dark stillness of the late afternoon. I dragged a heavy, black suitcase behind me.

As I unlocked the door something shifted in me. Dread settled deep in my gut as I pushed it open. Musty air hit me in a wave and I put a hand to my nose. After the weirdness of the lawn being mowed, I was relieved everything inside at least was exactly as it had been.

Dust had settled all over the furniture, and the curtains were still drawn. Photos of my parents and I adorned the wall of the hallway. I could almost hear the echo of my parents' voices, though my mother would never have let the place get so dusty. She was always such a clean freak. Mum suffered from terrible anxiety, and cleaning calmed her frayed nerves.

I set my suitcase down in the front room and walked through the downstairs. I wasn't really *seeing* anything, more just feeling it. The ghosts of my adolescence were everywhere. Every inch of the place was steeped in memories. Most were happy enough, but not all.

The kitchen was the hardest to face. It was the place Mum could always be found. I hadn't stepped foot in here since long before they died. In the decade since I'd left the psychiatric hospital, they had visited me in Harrogate far more often than

I'd made the effort to return here. The dining table still bore the worn patch where Dad's coffee mug used to sit every morning. Mum always placed it in the same spot. The clock on the wall had stopped at five thirty p.m., the time they always ate dinner. I stared at it. How could I ever clear this place out without drowning in the past?

The thought made my stomach turn. I returned to the front hallway, and a photo caught my eye. It hung on the wall at the bottom of the stairs. I stepped closer to take a proper look at it.

It was of my parents and me at a fair, but I didn't remember it being taken., and it wasn't hanging on the wall during my last visit.

I was a child in the photo. My parents and I stood in front of a merry-go-round ride. I had a large bundle of pink candy floss in my hand and a huge grin. I never remember being that happy. My parents rarely took me anywhere fun, let alone a fair. Mum didn't like crowds. She was always so scared of everything no matter how much Dad and I tried to convince her to let me go somewhere.

I ended up hating crowds just like she did. You never know who's watching.

Maybe the photo was from before I lost my memory, but Dad said the fire had destroyed all the photos from that time. And yet, here it was. I couldn't deny the young me staring back. I certainly didn't look any older than ten.

Dad looked so different. His smile in the photo wasn't the one I remembered. His hair was shaved, his eyes were harder somehow, and his grin was almost cruel. It made my stomach twist. The dad I knew had a warm, amiable smile, floppy brown hair, and was always the soft touch.

Mum wore her fake smile. It was the one she used when she

didn't like someone. Her gaze didn't meet the camera but the person taking the picture. Whoever it was, she didn't like them.

Why wasn't this photo dusty like the others? And why didn't I remember it?

I leaned in closer, squinting at the ride behind us. There was a reflection in the shiny red frame of the merry-go-round. It was the photographer.

They were crouched on their knees with the camera obscuring their face. Something about their posture and their presence felt unsettlingly familiar.

A chill crawled up the back of my neck, and I stepped away. My chest tightened. The house felt wrong. Like it wasn't just full of memories but something else entirely.

I shook my head. I was going crazy already. Maybe I couldn't stay here after all. Not right now. Not tonight.

So I bolted. I grabbed my suitcase and ran back outside. The freezing January air hit my cheeks and stole my breath. I'd get my credit card out and spend the night somewhere else. There was a Pocket Stay Hotel in town that always had small rooms at a good price. I knew there was enough money left on my newest credit card to book a room there for a few days until I was ready to face the house again.

As I locked the door behind me I glanced over at the neighbouring house. The curtains twitched, but no one came out. I wondered if they were the culprits behind the trimmed lawn as I turned back and tried to shake the chill from my spine.

It was just a house. I was being ridiculous. As I drove away, I checked the rearview mirror and caught one last glimpse of the house. The window with the twitching curtain next door was dark now, but I swore I saw the faintest shadow move just as I turned the corner.

Piper

After three days of putting up with cheap sausages and a lumpy mattress at the Pocket Stay Hotel, I revisited my parents' house with Adam the next weekend. The new job at Pinevale House was to begin on Monday, so it was then or never.

I determinedly plonked my belongings onto the dusty living room floor. The chill hit the back of my neck as soon as I entered, but Adam was unfazed. His relaxed presence made it easier to face somehow.

"Wow, this place is actually amazing!" he mused. "The rooms are enormous and the ceilings are so high. Maybe I was wrong. It's perfect, like it's been waiting for you."

His words made me nauseous, but he didn't notice. He grabbed a duster from the corner of the living room and started cleaning straight away. I pushed away the nerves and followed suit with my mum's old vacuum. An hour later, we'd cleared enough dust that he was helping me put some of my own belongings into the living room and the whole place was feeling a little less creepy. Maybe I could handle this after all.

When Adam wasn't looking, I stepped out into the back garden. The cool air brushed against my skin as I slid open the kitchen's patio doors. Overgrown bushes bordered the large space, except for the fence on the left-hand side, which separated it from the neighbour who'd been curtain-twitching the last time I was here.

Dad had loved to garden, and he had made the space beautiful. But it had been ignored since his death. Time had taken its toll on the plants and only weeds had survived. The smell of someone's wood burner drifted through the air, momentarily comforting. Maybe I could get one when the house was in a better state. Then my gaze fell on the neatly trimmed lawn and unease prickled at the back of my neck. The garden wasn't accessible without passing through the house, and yet someone had been out here mowing, too.

Did my parents give someone a key? Maybe a neighbour?

I hid behind one of the two enormous oak trees for a sneaky cigarette. As far as Adam was concerned, I'd quit months ago. It hadn't been a lie at the time. I did quit fully for a couple of months. Then there was the stress of the miscarriage. Add on a masked man shooting Evelyn dead right in front of me. After that, quitting didn't stand a chance.

I sucked the poison into my lungs and blew the smoke through my lips with a renewed sense of calm. I don't know why I bothered hiding it. It was rare I sparked up these days. And of course Adam would smell it on me. But he was too sweet to say anything. It was just easier to pretend I hadn't picked the habit back up.

The move had kicked my cravings into overdrive. Maybe this was a mistake. Maybe I was stepping back into a life that had already cost me my mind once.

A part of me couldn't believe the house was still sitting there waiting for me like a damn tomb. But all the things that had happened over the past few months had chipped away at who

I used to be. Then there was my debt and the eviction notices coming through the letterbox back at the flat. Another thing Adam didn't know about. I needed this house as much as I hated it.

At least it was on a quiet street. Though it was a bit too quiet for my tastes. I much preferred my apartment in Harrogate. It was simple and nowhere near as big, but on a busy-ish street and close to York city. I was alone, but I never felt alone. Then I met Adam.

I blew out one last puff of smoke and threw the cigarette butt on the ground, twisting my heel over it to make sure I'd stamped it out. I'd have to get a small bin out there, at least until I stopped again.

"You shouldn't do that."

The voice made me jump around so quickly that my hand connected with the trunk of the tree.

"Ouch!" I cried, shaking my sore hand. "Sorry, what?"

I looked toward the voice. An elderly man stared at me with narrow eyes. His head and shoulders loomed over the fence as if he was on a ladder. His sallow skin stretched taut across high cheekbones that seemed too sharp. Wiry white hair fell in uneven patches around his head, and his eyes were small and a bit too close together. They glinted as they fixed on me.

"Hi," I called out, my voice sounding much thinner than I'd intended. Something about the way he held himself creeped me out. It was the stillness in his shoulders and the oddly birdlike tilt of his head.

"I said, you shouldn't do that." He pointed to the ground where I'd extinguished my cigarette. He had a strange stiffness to him as though every movement required calculation. "It can start a fire."

"I made sure it was out," I replied with a smile. I didn't want to fall out with my neighbour on day one. He looked like he might die of old age any day now. "And it's not something I do often."

"Hmm." He raised a bushy white eyebrow at me.

"It's just stress from the move, that's all. I'm Piper."

"Yes. I know all about you."

"Oh," I replied, confused. "Who are you?"

"Typical," he muttered. "Norris Bale. I've lived here ever since you moved here as a kid."

I tried to place his face, but before I could say anything else, he disappeared. The sound of hard soles against metal rungs rang out.

How rude.

He'd clearly climbed a ladder to spy on me. I wasn't sure what was more creepy, using the ladder to look over the fence or him apparently knowing all about me. I didn't remember him, but I hadn't paid much attention in my teenage years. I thought hard, and a vague memory of someone old living next door came to me, but I couldn't remember their face.

Either way, something about him felt off, and I had the distinct impression he'd be watching me and Adam from his window for the rest of the day.

Shaking off the weirdness, I turned back to the patio doors and let myself in. The smell of dust hit me immediately from the house. It was still stale from being shut up for so long despite all of our dusting and vacuuming. I left the door open to let some much needed fresh air in.

I sighed and ran a hand through my loose hair. Adam would need to leave soon as he had to get home for work in the morning. His patients relied on him and he hated to let them down. His reliability was one of many things I loved about him. He was always there for anyone who needed him. Not like me.

Tomorrow, I'd start going through things and sorting out what to keep and what to get rid of. But for now I couldn't bring myself to face it. Adam was outside at the car grabbing the rest of the boxes.

I sank onto the couch. My exhausted body was grateful for the moment of quiet. The weight of the past few months bore down on me. Evelyn's death, the accusations, the piercing looks from people who seemed to know something I didn't. And then there was the baby.

I buried my face in my hands.

It had only been a few months since the miscarriage and I still hadn't processed it. I wasn't sure I ever would. It was easier to push it away and shove the pain into the furthest corner of my mind where it couldn't claw at me. But the thing about the past is that it doesn't stay buried. It creeps back no matter how hard you try to lock it out.

I straightened and forced myself upright. This week was supposed to be a new beginning. It was about a new job, a new town, and a fresh start.

A faint creak sounded from above, and I glanced up at the ceiling. Adam must have gone upstairs. I pushed myself off the couch and walked into the hallway.

"Adam?"

He didn't answer. Something definitely felt off. I climbed the stairs slowly, my steps echoing against the old wood. At the top of the landing, I paused and scanned the darkened hallway. The bathroom door was ajar, and I steeled myself before pushing it fully open.

Nothing.

Then I heard a faint thud from outside. Heart pounding, I moved to the window at the end of the hallway and peeked through the dusty glass. Adam was still outside at the car.

Wow, Piper. You're going crazy again already.

I let out a shaky breath and turned back towards the stairs. As I passed my parents' bedroom, I caught sight of a single photo frame lying face down on the dresser. I picked it up.

It was an old picture of me and my mother, and strangely warm to touch. It was another one I didn't recognise. There must have been more photos around than I realised. It wouldn't surprise me to find out Mum was keeping stuff from me. I always felt like she was keeping something big from me. We weren't exactly close, but I'd felt it in the quiet gaps of our conversations and the things she never said.

I looked a little older in this one, and my eyes held a sadness that made my stomach twist. My mother's hand rested on my shoulder, her smile unusually genuine this time. Dad wasn't in this one. He must have been taking the photo.

But what caught my attention wasn't any of us, it was the shadow in the corner. There was a figure, but it was blurred like it didn't belong in the picture. They were standing just beyond the garden gate. I pulled the photo closer, my pulse hammering. The moment I recognised him, my fingers jerked, and the frame crashed onto the dresser.

I knew that boy.

I had spent years trying to forget him.

Summer

The station was in its usual chaos for a Monday morning. Phones rang off the hook, conversations overlapped, and a steady stream of uniformed officers moved between desks. Summer stepped out of the open office and into the kitchen. Hunger gnawed at her again. She poured a glass of water, then grabbed a slice of toast for her second breakfast of the morning. The third trimester was relentless, and lately it felt like she was always eating just to keep up with it.

Her thoughts fell to Swanson. He'd been distant since his visit to Oakleigh House. She and Joshua had seen little of him. His mind was clearly on the missing Hayley Smith. Not that she cared. The poor girl needed someone looking out for her. She seemed to have no one except a made up boyfriend.

"Morning." Hart's voice pulled her from her thoughts.

Summer turned to see her leaning against the kitchen door frame with a coffee from a local shop in hand. Clearly she'd given up on the station's coffee machine. Her usual sharp grin was in place.

"Morning, Hart. How's your week going?"

"Uselessly so far, thanks for asking." Hart pushed off the frame and crossed the room. "I tried getting more out of the Oakleigh staff but no one had anything new to say. Apparently, Hayley was an angel who floated into work, did her job perfectly, and floated out again. No drama. No complaints. No bloody trace of her anywhere."

"That sucks." Summer offered a sympathetic smile.

"Understatement of the year." Hart let out a bitter laugh and took a sip of coffee. "Look, I was hoping you might help us with something. We need permission to speak to the patients at Oakleigh House. It's all vulnerable adult stuff, and Linda Reeve has been a nightmare about it."

"Linda's the manager, right?" Summer asked.

"Yeah, and she's not budging now without the go-ahead from their lead psychiatrist. Problem is, I haven't been able to get hold of him."

"Dr Andrew Metcalfe," Summer said, recalling the name Swanson had mentioned during their brief discussion about the case last night.

"That's him," Hart confirmed. "Swanson's in his office waiting to hear from the receptionist about the name on that note the guy handed us, Perry Vance, but in the meantime we're stuck. If you're free maybe you could work some of your psychologist magic and get us the green light?"

"Psychologist magic." Summer chuckled softly. "That's a new one."

"Don't make me beg." Hart grinned.

"I'll give them a call," Summer said as she reached for her phone. "Dr Metcalfe should understand the police are trying to help."

"You're a lifesaver, Summer." Hart's grin widened. "Here's the phone number."

Summer nodded and dialled the number for Oakleigh House

straight away. After a few rings, a brisk voice answered.

"Oakleigh House, how can I help you?"

"Good morning. This is Dr Summer Thomas. I'm calling on behalf of Derbyshire Police to request a conversation with Dr Metcalfe."

There was a pause, followed by the faint clatter of keys.

"Dr Metcalfe isn't in the building this morning. I can pass on a message and have him call you back this afternoon."

"That would be great. Please let him know it's urgent. It's regarding the Hayley Smith investigation and I need to speak with him today."

Summer left her contact details and ended the call, glancing up at Hart.

"Well?" Hart asked.

"They'll pass the message along. He should call me back later today."

"Well, let's hope he does." Hart crossed her fingers midair. "You'd be a star, Summer. Seriously."

"You can owe me dinner if I can sort it out," Summer replied, teasing.

"Deal," Hart said. "That baby is keeping you hungry these days, huh?"

She nodded down at the remaining piece of toast going cold on Summer's plate. Before Summer could respond, Swanson appeared in the doorway. His stoic face gave nothing away but his voice was urgent.

"Hart, we've got an address for this Perry Vance fella. Let's go."

"About bloody time." Hart straightened instantly, her coffee forgotten on the side.

"Bye, Summer," Swanson added quickly before he and Hart

disappeared into the corridor.

Summer stood as their footsteps faded down the hall, her glass of water still in hand. She felt the familiar tug of worry as Swanson disappeared out of sight. But then her phone buzzed in her pocket and pulled her attention away from them. She fished it out, half-expecting it to be a callback from Dr Metcalfe, but the screen showed an unknown number. She hesitated for a moment before swiping to answer.

"Dr Thomas speaking."

There was a brief crackle on the line, and then she heard a man's low, strained voice.

"Look into the staff at Oakleigh." The words tumbled out fast, like he only had seconds to say them.

"Who is this?" Summer froze, her grip tightening around the phone.

But there was only silence. Then a click as the call disconnected.

Piper

A dam returned home Sunday morning, and the rest of the weekend passed without incident. Except for a couple of sleepless nights.

I couldn't return to my old room as Mum had turned it into a sewing room. So after a brief attempt at sleeping in their bed, I slept in the spare room. I didn't see Norris Bale again, though in fairness I didn't venture outside often. Yet when Monday morning came and it was time to start my new job at Pinevale House, I felt sick to my stomach.

My hands trembled as I parked on the street outside Pinevale. I ignored its cramped driveway, which stretched toward the back of the property and felt too enclosed. Instead, I chose the open street.

I stared up at the old brick building through the windscreen. It was so much smaller than the enormous secure hospital I used to work at in Harrogate, but when I climbed out of the car and approached the front door, that eerie institutional feel was still there.

Despite it being a less secure home than the hospital, the front door was still very much locked to most patients—or clients as staff referred to them in these places. Sue Welsh, my new manager, had already explained to me in the interview that clients had to "earn" a key by showing positive behaviours. The whole point of these halfway homes was to prepare people for living alone again. Once they earned their key, they got to come and go from the home almost as much as they pleased.

As a new member of staff, I didn't yet have a key. So I pressed the bell to the right of the front door. It opened automatically, someone had clearly seen me on camera and buzzed it open without using the intercom to check who I was. Great security. Though the hospital wasn't much better, now I think of it.

Few people try to sneak inside these places. They only ever try to get out in my experience, and even that wasn't hard. They earned a day out with the staff, then ran away when no one was looking.

The air seemed heavier as I stepped through the front door, like the building itself was closing in on me. I spotted Sue waiting for me as soon as I walked in. Her bright bottle-red hair was hard to miss. It fell to her shoulders and framed a face lined with years of stress and sleepless nights. Her sharp eyes were magnified slightly by her glasses, and they gave her an air of quiet authority. Though the tight smile she offered didn't quite reach her eyes.

"Hi, Sue," I said with the brightest smile I could manage to hide my nerves.

"Hi! Good to see you again, Piper," she said as she glanced at her watch. "Let's get you settled in."

We made small talk about the weather and my move to Derby as I followed her down the narrow corridor. My new trainers squeaked annoyingly against the polished floors. At least they were clean.

It was quieter than I'd expected, particularly when compared to the hospital. There were no alarms blaring, and no raised voices or constant chatter. The TV was turned off. There was just an inaudible murmur coming from somewhere deeper in the building. It almost felt too calm.

Sue began the tour. She told me about the six large, en-suite bedrooms upstairs which spanned two floors. Each room had its own pale wooden door and small brass number plate. The enormous kitchen had spotless counters and a large table in the centre, surrounded by mismatched chairs that gave it a homely but slightly haphazard feel.

She explained that the roomy living area, filled with well-worn sofas and a scattering of magazines on the coffee table, was where the patients spent most of their time, though it was empty at that point. The faint scent of furniture polish lingered.

There were two lone apartments in the back garden. They were visible through the wide kitchen window. Their grey brick exteriors and small, curtained windows looked oddly detached from the rest of the house.

"We use those for patients transitioning to independent living," she explained. Her tone was clipped, like she'd given the same tour a thousand times before.

I nodded as I tried to keep track of everything she was saying, but my mind kept drifting. It was hard to focus on anything since Evelyn's death. And I didn't really know what to expect from this job, but it was already a world away from the violent chaos I was used to.

Which was exactly the point, I reminded myself. I needed something easier with less violence. Yet I somehow felt out of my depth in this quiet space. At least in the old place I felt sane compared to the patients. I wasn't sure it would be the same at Pinevale.

"Time for you to meet the patients!" Sue said as she climbed back up the stairs to the first floor. "We like to keep them busy. So some of them are out right now working on the allotments nearby, but I'll introduce you to the ones who are here. This is Lily's room. She's eighteen years old. Been struggling with anorexia for a while now and is very nervous of strangers. Sweet girl, though. Very quiet."

Sue stopped outside bedroom three and knocked lightly before pushing the door open. Inside, a thin, pale girl sat on a double bed. She wrapped both arms tightly around her knees as we walked in. Lank, brown hair fell down to her waist. She looked up at me with wide, scared eyes, and I felt a pang of sympathy in my chest.

"Lily, this is Piper. Our newest team member."

Lily gave me a small, hesitant smile. I tried to return it, but my heart sank as I took in her fragile frame. She looked like she might shatter if someone breathed too hard around her. I said a soft hello, not wanting to overwhelm her. Sue quickly ushered me back into the hallway. Her voice lowered to a more serious tone.

"We do our best with her but she's resistant to treatment. Not much we can do until she wants to help herself."

"Shouldn't she be on an eating disorder ward?" I asked.

"Sure she should, but there's no room anywhere."

I nodded again, feeling that heaviness in my chest grow. I'd seen patients with anorexia before, but never to Lily's extreme.

The next patient we visited was a woman in her fifties. As Sue opened the door, we found her pacing the floor of her bedroom mumbling to herself. Her dishevelled, brown hair was streaked with grey, and there was a nervous energy in the way she moved.

"Margaret," Sue said, raising her voice slightly to get the woman's attention. "This is Piper. She's new here."

Margaret stopped pacing immediately and turned to me, her brow furrowed.

"Did I lock the door?" she asked. Then continued pacing without waiting for a response. "Where's my cup? I had it just a minute ago. Did I lock the door?"

"It might look like a memory issue but she actually has severe anxiety," Sue explained to me quietly as Margaret began a search of her wardrobe. "She tries to keep everything under control, but it's hard for her."

Margaret stopped and turned to stare at us, her eyes flitted between us as if she'd already forgotten what she'd just asked. I offered her a quick hello and a nod, and we moved on.

"She also lies a lot so take what she says with a pinch of salt," Sue whispered as we walked away.

"Oh dear," I replied.

The third patient was another middle-aged woman sitting calmly on the edge of her bed. Her frizzy, untamed hair stuck out in wild angles, as though it had resisted every brush that ever came near it. Despite this, there was an air of deliberate composure about her. She folded her hands neatly in her lap, and her posture was perfectly straight. As we entered, she looked up with a bright, almost childlike smile that lit up her pale, round face.

"And this is our Samantha," Sue said, her tone bright once again. "Samantha, this is Piper. Our newest team member."

"Hello, dears," Samantha said cheerfully in a foreign accent I couldn't quite place. "Lovely to meet you. Do you want to play chess with me, Piper?"

"Later, Samantha," Sue replied for me. "I need to show Piper around right now."

Samantha's smile faltered for a second before she regained her composure. There was something off about the way her expression shifted so quickly. It was like a mask slipping back into place. Sue closed the door and leaned closer to me.

"She claims to have that multiple personality disorder or whatever it's called these days," She trailed off and gave me a pointed look.

"Dissociative Identity Disorder," I automatically replied.

"Sorry?"

"Dissociative Identity Disorder. That's what it's called these days."

"Oh, well. Whatever it's called she's likely faking it seeing as so many specialists say it doesn't exist."

I wanted to argue with her, but thought it best to keep my mouth shut on my first day. We continued the tour and eventually Sue led me out to the garden. The two small apartments she'd pointed out earlier stood side by side and were slightly apart from the main building. Their windows looked out facing the main house with a view of the neat lawn and patio area. It was much nicer than my parents' back garden with its dead plants everywhere.

"As I said, this is where we house the long-term patients who are getting ready to transition to live on their own," Sue said, stopping in front of the first apartment. "Bella lives here. She's in her thirties, has autism, and severe anxiety but she's managed to get it under control. She's doing well."

I nodded as I peered through the window. I couldn't see much but the place looked tidy enough. Bella wasn't in from what I could tell, and Sue didn't offer to introduce me to her, so we moved on to the next apartment.

"And here," she said, her voice dropping, "is where Peter lives."

There was a tension in her voice when she said his name, and I frowned, glancing at her.

"Peter?"

"He's different from the others," she said as her eyes shifted away from mine. "You'll meet him soon enough."

I didn't ask for more. I'd find out on my own, eventually. Sue spent the rest of the morning going over paperwork and general procedures, and in the afternoon we had a break for lunch. I wandered outside for some air.

I felt calmer. Everything had gone well so far, but taking in so much new information over the course of the day pressed down on me, and I needed a minute to collect myself.

As I walked past Peter's apartment to the shared patient and staff smoking area—which you'd never find in a secure hospital—I glimpsed a man standing in the doorway staring at me as I walked. He was older than I expected, maybe in his fifties, and tall with a broad frame that filled the doorway. His dark eyes followed me as I moved past him, and something about his gaze made the hairs on the back of my neck stand on end. His face was utterly blank as if he was waiting for a reaction.

"Hi," I said awkwardly, stopping for a second.

He didn't respond. His face was completely devoid of expression. I felt an uncomfortable knot twist in my stomach. After being used to working with some of the most dangerously ill patients in the country back in Harrogate, that didn't happen often.

"Well, have a good day," I muttered, walking away quickly. I didn't look back, but I could still feel his eyes on me long after

I turned the corner.

When I returned to the office after my break, Sue was at her desk flipping through some papers. She barely glanced up when I came in.

"How's lunch going so far?" she asked in a distant voice.

"Fine," I said, though I wasn't sure that was true. "I met Peter."

"Did you?" Sue's hand froze mid-page turn, but she didn't look up.

"Yeah. He didn't say much. Just stared at me."

"He does that when he's in a mood. You'll get used to it." She let out a short, humourless laugh.

I didn't like the sound of that, but before I could ask more Sue slid a stack of patient files toward me.

"You should spend some time going through these," she said, her tone suddenly brisk. "It'll give you a better sense of who you're working with."

I hesitated, feeling the weight of the files under my hands.

"Is there anything I should know about Peter?"

Sue paused, then shook her head, her expression unreadable.

"Nothing in particular. His history is all in the files."

So I spent the next hour reading through patient backgrounds. I read about the breakdown of Margaret's marriage and how the death of her child pushed her already fragile mind over the edge. I read about Lily's horrific childhood abuse and her constant struggle with food since the age of nine. Then I found out who Peter really was.

The words on the page felt like they were burning into my brain. Peter was a convicted rapist. Doctors diagnosed him with antisocial personality disorder. He'd been in a ward like I used to work on for over a decade before moving to Pinevale

House two years ago. The most recent doctor's note from the psychiatrist who ran Pinevale stated Peter was almost ready to live alone with frequent visits from carers to ensure he stayed stable and took his medication.

It was one thing working with dangerous patients in a hospital surrounded by security. I never really thought about how it would be to work with one in a place like this. What happened to them after the hospital had never really crossed my mind.

I moved on to the next patient and finished reading the files as the day ended. I felt more drained than ever as I said goodbye to Sue and reassured her I'd had a great first day. As I walked to my car, the evening air felt thick with tension. I just wanted to go home and take a shower.

As I stepped onto the pavement, the air felt too still. The car park was nearly deserted, but something prickled at the back of my neck like I was being watched. I turned my head just slightly to scan the street, but there was no one there.

As I approached my car something caught my eye. There was a piece of paper stuck under the windscreen wipers. Frowning, I pulled it free and unfolded it. Someone had scrawled a message in messy handwriting that I didn't recognise. The last time someone had left a note on my car it was someone moaning about parking outside of their house. Not this time.

My eyes darted over the jagged handwriting as I tried to process the words. But the moment I read them, my blood turned to ice.

The Shadow

Hello, beautiful.

I've missed you. I knew you'd come back. I've been waiting. It's been too long, but I'm close now. Closer than you might think.

I know the world hasn't been kind to you. They have lied to you. Twisted you. Bent you into something small, something breakable. But I see you. I always have. I see you when no one else does.

I know what they did to you. I know how they made you doubt yourself, how they buried the truth so deep inside your mind that you forgot. But it's still there. The real you is still there. I wonder... do you feel it yet? That itch at the back of your skull? The feeling that something isn't right, that you're standing in the wrong place, living the wrong life?

You are.

But I can fix it.

You don't have to be afraid anymore. I won't let them touch you. They won't whisper behind your back, won't twist your thoughts, won't make you doubt yourself. They won't hurt you—not while I'm here.

And if they try?

I will make them bleed for you.

I want you to know something, something they've kept from you. You belong here. With me. You always have. That truth is still inside you, buried under the lies they forced into your head. But it's waiting to come back, waiting to wake up.

And soon, you will remember.

You won't have to wonder who you are anymore. You won't have to be alone.

I've never left you.

All these years, I've been watching. Keeping you safe. Even when you ran away, even when they tried to lock me out of your life, I stayed close. You were never as alone as you thought. I was there. I was always there.

Do you remember the time you thought someone was following you home? The flicker of movement in the corner of your eye? The way you swore you heard footsteps when no one was there?

That was me.

Not to scare you. Never to scare you. Only to protect you.

You don't have to be afraid, not of me. I've seen the way they look at you. I know what they think, what they whisper behind closed doors. But I won't let them take anything else from you. I won't let them fill your head with their poison.

I know the truth. And soon, you will too.

You don't remember me yet, but that's okay. You belong to me. You always have. That truth is still inside you, waiting to wake up.

And soon, you will remember.

Soon, you will see.

We'll see each other soon. Sooner than you think.

You'll see.

Piper

The letter sat on the passenger seat. I'd folded it back up as if hiding the words might lessen its power. Yet its presence filled the car like a living thing. The final words kept running through my brain.

You'll see.

I kept my eyes on the building in my rearview mirror as my fingers clenched the steering wheel. Who would write something like that? No one came to mind, yet an unshakable sense of familiarity crept in that I couldn't place. The letters seemed so familiar.

I scanned the parking lot one last time as I locked all the car doors with a quick press of the button. The sharp click echoed in the silence. The stillness of the night felt heavy. Part of me half-expected someone to jump out from behind the bushes. Peter, maybe. Or Margaret asking me where something was.

A flicker of movement in the top window of Pinevale House caught my attention as I shifted the car into reverse. A pale face pressed against the glass of a bedroom window just visible in the evening's last light. *Lily.*

She looked down at me like she was watching me. Or like she knew something. Maybe she'd written the note.

A chill crawled over my skin and prickled down my neck. I

tore my eyes away as my heart hammered in my chest. I gripped the wheel until my knuckles turned white.

I was being ridiculous. I could feel my thoughts unravelling. Their delicate threads frayed at the edges in the same way they had right before my parents locked me away on a psych ward. I was jumping to conclusions assuming a sweet girl with anorexia was watching me or leaving weird notes.

The psychology student in me whispered that this was simply classic projection. It was nothing more than my mind grasping for something tangible to fear in the face of so many bad things happening in such a brief time.

With a shaking hand, I picked up my phone and dialled Adam. He'd know what to say. It was turning out to be useful being in love with a therapist. Thanks to so much happening in the past year since we met, he already knew me better than anyone. He was so easy to open up to about my past. I'd never met anyone I could talk to like him. He answered on the second ring.

"Adam," I said, my voice shaking. "You'll never believe what I just found on my car."

"Hey, Piper. What's going on? Are you alright?"

I told him about the note and read out every unsettling word of it as my voice trembled. There was silence on the other end, and I could picture the way his face would screw up as he tried to make sense of it. He'd be as disturbed as I was.

"It sounds like someone's playing a prank," he said, but I could hear the underlying tension. "Could they be a patient with a bit too much time on their hands?"

"Yes. Probably," I said, gripping the wheel even tighter. "I'll tell Sue tomorrow and see what she thinks, but it's creepy, right? You don't think it's just me overthinking it?"

"No, I don't think you're overthinking it," he said firmly.

"But that's probably the best explanation for now. Stay calm. Just keep it all in perspective."

I nodded, even though he couldn't see me. The familiarity of his steady voice helped to keep me from spiralling too badly. I knew he was probably right. Patients with mental health issues sometimes did odd things; dealing with that was just part of the job. A male patient with a history of stalking had actually written me a letter before. I'd laughed that one off.

But with being unable to remember such a large part of my previous life in Derby, my biggest fear was always that I'd forgotten something, or someone, important. This letter played on that exact fear perfectly.

"Keep me on speaker while you're driving home," he suggested. "I can help you focus."

"Thanks, Adam." I took a deep breath. Then set the phone down and switched it to speaker mode. "I didn't realise how much this job might get to me. I thought it would be easy after the hospital."

"It's only because it's all new to you. It'll settle down," he reassured me. "This is only the beginning and you're still adjusting. Take it easy on yourself. And tomorrow, tell Sue everything. She'll know what to do if this sort of thing happens. I bet one of the patients is known for playing silly pranks. Or there is a dodgy neighbour she forgot to mention."

I drove slowly. My eyes flitted between the road ahead and the rearview mirror. Every pair of headlights felt like they were getting closer and lingering too long behind me before eventually turning away. By the time I pulled up in front of my parents' house, my shoulders ached from the tension and my eyes were sore with fatigue.

"You made it," Adam's gentle voice came through the

speaker.

"Yes," I said, trying to sound relieved. "Thanks for staying with me."

"Anytime," he said. "Get some rest and don't let it get to you too much. Tomorrow's a new day."

I ended the call with the letter's words still pressing on me. My parents' street was silent. The house loomed over me like something from a nightmare. I glanced over at the letter again, still folded neatly on the passenger seat. It called to me, pulling me back to those scrawled, jagged words.

You're safe now. I'm here, watching over you.

I turned my gaze to the rearview mirror. My breath hitched as I glimpsed something. A figure in the dark? I blinked, but it was gone.

Just your mind.

But dread seeped through every inch of me. With a deep breath, I grabbed the letter, stuffed it into my bag, and hurried inside. I slammed the door shut with a bang behind me and locked it up, double, then triple checking that the door would not open.

But even as I turned on every light downstairs there was still a coldness. A feeling I couldn't shake that whoever had written that letter, wasn't done with me yet.

Swanson

The rush hour traffic was even worse than Swanson had expected. What should have been a quick drive from Derby to Kirk Hallam turned into a slow crawl, the streets choked with cars, buses, and impatient drivers who honked at every slight delay. Swanson drummed the steering wheel with his forefinger impatiently while Hart shifted uncomfortably in the passenger seat. Her coffee cup was now empty and forgotten in the cupholder.

"Second time's the charm, eh?" Hart quipped, but frustration dulled her usual sharp humour.

"If we'd got this over with this morning, we wouldn't be stuck in this mess," Swanson muttered. This was the second time they'd tried to visit Perry Vance with the address that they had on file for him. No one had answered the earlier knock on the door.

"You know people don't always stick to the schedules we need them to." Hart raised an eyebrow at him. "Besides, you love an excuse to grumble."

"Who doesn't love a good grumble?" Swanson smirked. "You certainly do."

"I'll admit I don't have high hopes for this visit," Hart admitted. "But let's see what he's got."

63

By the time they reached Perry Vance's address, dusk had settled over the modest estate on the outskirts of Ilkeston. The rows of semi-detached houses were all unusually large, with long driveways and barely any similarities between them. But Perry Vance's address stood out thanks to the peeling paint on the door and litter scattered across his overgrown front garden.

"Ready?" Swanson parked the car on the uneven curb and exchanged a glance with Hart.

"Always," she said as she unbuckled her seatbelt.

They walked up the cracked path side by side. Swanson's shoes crunched against stray gravel as he watched the faded curtains drawn tightly across the downstairs windows. The air was damp and made his skin feel clammy. He knocked firmly on the faded white door.

There was nothing at first, no sound and no movement. Swanson was about to knock again when the curtain at the front window twitched. He caught a brief glimpse of a gaunt face before the fabric fell back into place.

"Someone's home," Hart said under her breath.

A second later, the door creaked open a crack. Swanson stiffened. The same guy who had handed them the piece of paper peeked through the gap. He forced his face to stay neutral, but a flicker of confusion tightened his jaw. He hadn't expected to see the same guy. Was this Perry Vance? That made no sense.

If this guy was Perry, why the hell hadn't he spoken to them outside Oakleigh? Why the cryptic message? He could have just spoken to them then and there rather than playing games. Swanson shifted his weight. The deadbolt was still engaged. The man had called them here, but now his frame was half-hidden behind the door, like he wasn't sure if he wanted them to step inside.

His sunken eyes darted between Swanson and Hart as if he wasn't entirely sure they were real. The dark circles beneath them were like bruises, as if he hadn't slept in days. His clothes were rumpled and his thin, greasy hair stuck up in all directions.

"Mr Vance?" Swanson asked, ignoring the stench of sweat and grease coming from the property.

The man didn't respond right away. His gaze lingered on Hart for a second too long before moving back to Swanson.

"Who are you?" he asked.

"Detective Inspector Alex Swanson, Derbyshire Police. This is my colleague DI Rebecca Hart. Are you Perry Vance?"

"Yes." His eyes flicked past them both as he scanned the street like he expected someone to appear.

"We spoke to you briefly outside Oakleigh House yesterday." Swanson's eyes narrowed as he studied Perry's reaction. "You gave us a note."

"No, I didn't." Perry's face twisted in confusion.

"Pretty sure you did," Hart interjected sharply. "We're here to follow up on that and to ask you about Hayley Smith."

The mention of Hayley's name made Perry flinch. He stepped back slightly, gripping the edge of the door like it was the only thing holding him up.

"Sometimes I do things I can't remember," he said, his voice rising in panic. "But I know nothing about Hayley Smith disappearing."

"Then why give us your name?" Swanson pressed.

"I don't remember!" Perry's voice cracked. His eyes darted nervously between them. "I know nothing. You've got it wrong. It was nothing to do with me, she just knew too much."

65

"Well, you seem to know something about her, Perry," Hart said, taking a small step forward. "What do you mean she knew too much?"

"I meant nothing." Perry's voice dropped to a whisper, and he glanced over his shoulder as if expecting someone to be standing behind him. "She was nosy, that's all. Always asking questions, always prying. It's why she—"

He halted. His lips pressed into a thin line.

"Why she what?" Swanson asked in a harder tone.

Perry shook his head, his eyes wide with fear. "I've already said too much. You need to go. Now."

"Perry, if you know something about Hayley's disappearance, we need you to tell us," Hart said firmly.

"I said, leave!" Perry's voice rose, and he slammed the door shut with surprising force.

Swanson and Hart exchanged a look. Neither of them moved right away. The faint sound of Perry's muffled voice came from behind the door, but it was impossible to make out what he was saying.

"Well, that was enlightening," Hart said dryly. "I don't think he liked you."

"He's hiding something," Swanson said as he stepped back from the door. "I think he knows exactly what's happened to Hayley."

"Think he's scared to tell us? Or just crazy?" Hart asked as they made their way back to the car.

"Well, he definitely has issues if he doesn't remember giving us his name." Swanson opened the driver's side door and slid in. "I assume he's scared too. But scared of what? That is the question we need to know."

"He could be scared of himself. What if a part of him wanted to hand himself in? Maybe he's our guy."

"Maybe."

As they drove away, Swanson couldn't shake the image of Perry's haunted, terrified eyes. He glanced back at the house in the rearview mirror, just in time to see Perry frantically closing the curtains on the top floor. The man was clearly terrified of something. They just had to find out what.

Piper

The dream started as they always did. Slow, hazy shapes drifted in and out of the shadows. I was ten years old again and my brown hair reached all the way down to my belly button. I wandered down endless dark corridors as each corner twisted into another. The smell of burning was so strong it stung the inside of my nose. The walls stood tall and loomed over my small stature, but they didn't scare me.

Then I saw him. The boy who was faceless but somehow familiar. He stood at the end of the hall and reached out. His arm stretched across the void between us. My feet closed the rest of the gap and when my hand found his, a wave of warmth spread over my skin. But as he led me forward, that warmth turned to a searing pain.

A fire flared to life in the darkness. Its glow lit up the charred wood as smoke billowed up into the black. My pulse thundered as the boy's grip grew tighter and pulled me toward the blaze. I couldn't make out his face, but I welcomed the familiarity in his touch. There was no escaping him. I didn't even want to escape him. I'd follow him anywhere.

He forced us to move so close that the flames licked at my arms and wrists and made me scream in pain.

I jolted awake with a gasp, My hands scratched at the uneven skin on my forearm. The old burn scars that snaked around my right wrist and up my arm prickled as if they were fresh wounds. They were always the same after the dreams.

I threw off the covers and stared at the pale marks winding up my arms. The scars were still slightly pink even after eighteen years had passed, and my fingertips brushed over them as I tried to steady my breath.

I stumbled to the bathroom. The harsh light made everything sharper and eased away the remnants of the dream that still clung to my skin. I leaned over the sink and splashed cold water on my face, letting the droplets sting my skin awake.

It took me another minute to remember it was Tuesday, and I had to be at work for nine. It was almost six twenty a.m., so I busied myself with the mundane ritual of showering, cleaning teeth, and getting dressed. I made sure I wasn't wearing any jewellery and pulled my hair back into a tight bun, although I probably didn't need to. It was a habit from the hospital. Evelyn had made them mandatory after too many patients yanked ponytails during restraints. By the time I was finished, the nightmare had slipped away enough that I felt normal again.

Downstairs I spotted the letter on the kitchen table. It was folded up just as I'd left it last night. Its jagged scrawl burned into my mind, though I felt less freaked out by it this morning. It was just a stupid note. I picked it up and tucked it into my bag, ready to get answers from Sue.

The drive to work was short, and when the receptionist buzzed me into Pinevale, Sue was in the office. She sat at her desk shuffling through a stack of patient files, and she'd pulled her red hair back into a messy bun with a black clip. She glanced up with her usual stern expression and peered at me with her dark eyes. She'd seemed so much friendlier during the job interview.

"Morning, Piper," she said before looking back down at the paperwork.

"Morning, Sue." I shifted uncomfortably, wondering if she'd laugh me off, or worse, think I was overreacting. "I, um, found something stuck on my car last night. A note."

"What sort of note?" Sue looked up, her brow furrowed.

"It says someone is watching me." I handed her the letter.

Her eyes scanned over it, and I watched as her frown deepened. I caught a flash of something like concern, but it vanished as quickly as it appeared.

"And you think this is from a patient?" Her voice held a warning edge.

"Well, I wasn't sure," I replied, backtracking slightly.

I'd expected her to laugh and tell me something like Lily does this all the time or that Margaret enjoys leaving random letters around that make no sense. I didn't expect her to sound annoyed with me.

"Piper, we're severely understaffed today. I need to sort that out and not worry about silly notes or accusations against the patients."

"Sorry. I just thought it was odd, that's all. I didn't mean to accuse anyone. The way it's written is strange, like the writer's thoughts are not coherent. I don't recognise the handwriting."

"I get the letter is weird, but I don't want you jumping to conclusions on your second day here." She cut me off, folded the paper briskly, and handed it back. "Our patients already face enough stigma just for living here. The neighbours keep finding excuses to complain, and if they think our residents are causing trouble it'll only get worse."

"I understand." I nodded. Though the tension between us tightened like a rope. "I'm sorry if it came across that way."

"Look, it's likely nothing." Sue's expression softened a fraction. "It doesn't even have your name on it. It could have been a mistake. Maybe it was meant for someone else, or some busybody neighbour left it looking for attention or looking to cause us trouble."

"You're probably right," I agreed, trying to ignore the strange knot in my stomach. "I didn't mean to suggest anything. It's just unsettling."

"Of course. Just try not to let it get to you, alright? Focus on work. The patients need us and we certainly don't have time for any extra drama. There's enough in this house as it is! Wait until you try telling Margaret she can't have a takeaway three nights in a row."

I nodded and tucked the letter back into my bag. There was clearly no point pressing her further. Sue had made her stance clear. But even as I returned to my tasks, her dismissive reaction gnawed at me.

Maybe she was right and it was just a mistake or some harmless mix-up. But when I left the office, the image of that faceless boy and the flames stayed like an aftertaste I couldn't quite shake.

As I stepped back out into the corridor, I spotted a pale face down the hall partially hidden behind a curtain of greasy brown hair.

Lily.

The way she watched me made my skin prickle. The office door wasn't closed while we were speaking, she must have heard my conversation with Sue about the letter. Just as I opened my mouth to greet her, she ducked around the corner and disappeared.

"Lily?" I called, my voice echoing down the hall.

I hurried after her and rounded the corner just in time to see her disappear into her room. I followed and knocked lightly on the door before pushing it open. Lily sat cross-legged on her bed drawing in her sketch pad. Her pencil scratched rhythmically against the page. I caught a glimpse of the lines. They were chaotic and resembled nothing I recognised. She stared up at me with an expression I couldn't read.

"Were you listening to me and Sue just now?" I asked gently.

"I heard you talking," she said quietly.

"What did you hear?" I pushed.

She didn't respond. After a moment of silence, she looked down and fiddled with the edge of her sleeve.

"I just wanted to check if you were okay," I tried again. Still nothing, I clearly wasn't going to get anything out of her. I forced a smile and backed out of the room. "I'll check on you later."

As I turned to leave, I felt her eyes following me. Lily knew more than she'd let on, but I'd need to gain her trust first.

I walked to the living room to say good morning to the other patients. The fire from my nightmare seared vividly in my mind. The sharp, acrid scent of burning filled my nose, so real it made my breath hitch. I blinked and it was gone. But the letter's words still echoed in my head. The messy parts of my life were twisting together, and whoever was pulling the threads was getting closer.

Summer

After nearly a year as a forensic psychologist with the police, the station felt like a second home. It helped that Swanson and Hart practically lived there.

Summer still wasn't used to how the place could swing from deafening noise to eerie silence depending on the case. Today was one of the quiet days. Most officers were out in the field, chasing down leads on Hayley Smith. Even DCI Jane Murray had left her office to help in the field, which was rare. Hart must have been a good influence on her.

Summer traced the edges of the file in front of her as her thoughts focused on the baby growing inside of her. She had sworn she wouldn't have another child without being married first. Yet here she was having one with Alex Swanson, the same man who'd been terrified enough just to move in with her. She smiled. He was going to be a fantastic dad.

Her phone buzzed, breaking her out of her thoughts. A message from Swanson popped up: *Everything okay? Need anything?*

Summer smiled. He'd been hovering like an overprotective mother hen ever since she told him about the weird phone call. For a man who barely knew how to express concern with words, he was doing his best.

Just working in the office. You good?

Her phone pinged again.

Good. Don't overdo it, yeah? I'm nipping out.

She chuckled, shaking her head. Swanson could spend hours chasing down murderers without breaking a sweat, but her being alone in the office for an afternoon apparently required constant check-ins.

Yes, Dad. I'll be careful sitting at my desk.

She smirked as she hit send, imagining the grumble she'd get in response. Just as she was about to return to her file about a streaker, her phone rang. She picked it up quickly, expecting Swanson to complain about her sarcasm. But it wasn't him.

"Summer Thomas."

"Summer." Hart's voice was urgent. "I need you to come with me while Swanson is out on another lead. There's a man called Perry Vance who I think knows what happened to Hayley Smith. He's paranoid, and I want you there to assess him. Not officially. Just whether he's got mental health issues or if he's telling the truth. It'll take ages to get him assessed officially. This is just a quick visit to check on him."

"Without Swanson?" Summer asked.

"Yes, without him. Vance is all over the place. I'd love your professional opinion, and also I don't think he likes men. Swanson's presence really freaked him out before. It's in Kirkhallam."

Summer glanced at the clock. She still had some time before she had to pick up Joshua from her mum's place, and Mum only lived five minutes away from Kirkhallam so it was on the way.

"I'll drive separately and meet you there. Text me the address." She grabbed her coat and keys. "See you soon."

It didn't take long to get to Kirk Hallam. When Summer arrived at the narrow terraced house on a quiet street, she spotted Hart's car parked at an awkward angle out front. Of course. The woman never parked straight. Summer smirked to herself. Swanson always said Hart treated parking like a creative expression rather than a functional necessity.

Hart climbed out of the car and greeted her with a curt nod. "You took your time."

"I did the legal speed limits, actually." Summer raised an eyebrow.

"You and your law-abiding ways." Hart snorted. She gestured toward the house with her thumb. "Let's get this over with. Just stay close to me. This guy's on edge and Swanson will kill me if you get hurt."

Summer followed her up the driveway, rolling her eyes. "You two worry too much. I know how to handle an unstable man."

Hart shot her a sideways glance.

"Okay, maybe not perfectly," Summer admitted. "One did stab me in the neck. But hey, I lived."

"Yeah, let's not make that a pattern." Hart sighed as she rapped her knuckles against the door.

It opened almost immediately. The man standing there looked older than Summer had expected. He was tall and thin, his hair unkempt, eyes wide and darting around like he expected someone to jump out at him. Then his gaze landed on Hart. He went still.

"No. You need to leave. I can't talk to you," he said in a voice that was oddly familiar. His hand trembled as he wiped it across his face. "I told you already."

"You do remember me from yesterday then, Perry?" Hart asked.

He nodded. "But I remember things that didn't happen sometimes. I hear things. And people are following me. It's dangerous. You need to leave."

Hart stepped forward calmly. "We're here to help, Perry. We just need you to tell us everything you know. Start from the beginning."

Summer kept a careful distance, letting Hart take the lead while she observed. She studied his body language and his nervous tics. He was clearly struggling with his mental health. His eyes flicked to Summer, and his breath caught in his throat.

"You shouldn't be here." He took a step back and shook his head.

"What can you tell me about Hayley?" Hart brought his attention back to her.

"She's gone, isn't she?" he muttered as he focused his gaze back on her. "Hayley. They won't find her. I saw her. She used to visit me. But now she's not coming back. She's not coming back."

"When did she last visit you, Perry?" Hart asked.

"I tried to warn her. But she wouldn't listen." His hands clenched at his sides.

"Who do you mean?" Hart's voice was sharp.

"I saw her talking to him. Then he said he was coming for her." His voice was becoming more frantic. "And then she was gone."

"Who was she talking to?" Summer stepped forward, intrigued.

"A man," he whispered. His eyes locked onto Summer's with wide pupils. "You know. Don't you? He knows you."

"Who? Can you remember anything else?" she asked softly.

"I don't know. I'm not sure what exactly happened. But

I swear I wasn't imagining it. Hayley was real. She came to make sure I was okay in her purple shirts. She was talking to me before she disappeared."

His hands wrung together, his expression twisted with desperation. Summer shared a glance with Hart, who nodded subtly.

"Perry, we'll have someone check in with you later. Just try to stay calm. We'll be in touch."

Outside, Hart turned to her, her voice low.

"What do you think?"

Summer took a moment before answering.

"I don't know. He's clearly spooked by something, but he's also very unwell. I'm guessing Oakleigh is the type of home where they also visit people in the community?"

"What do you mean?"

"Some homes have clients in the house and also in the community. They visit them to make sure they're okay once they leave the home."

"So Hayley probably visited him as a part of her job? That would make sense. Did the head psychiatrist get back to you yesterday?"

Summer shook her head. "Not yet. I'll call him first thing tomorrow."

"Fine. If he doesn't call, then Swanson and I will visit again. You might need to come with us."

"Sure."

Hart yelled goodbye as she stood next to her car, refusing to get in until Summer was safely inside her own.

Summer fastened her seatbelt, ready to pull away, when something stopped her cold. Perry's voice wasn't just familiar. She'd heard it before. Her stomach turned. It was him.

"Look into the staff at Oakleigh."

Piper

The rest of the day passed in a bit of a blur, but without incident. A lot of the clients, including Lily, went out to a pottery farm with the other staff. I volunteered to stay behind with Sue and the three patients who didn't want to go.

Margaret was too anxious to leave the house and instead followed me around, repeatedly asking if I was new. The other staff found her constant questions frustrating but I didn't mind. There was something heartbreakingly sweet about her, like she was trying to anchor herself to something familiar but kept forgetting how to do it. She was so lost after her breakdown, it was unsettling to see. That kind of loss of identity terrified me.

Maybe that's why I liked her the most, even though we weren't supposed to have favourites. I could relate. That could've been me. Hell, it still could be if I didn't get my act together.

At the end of the shift at six p.m., the drive home felt heavy, and I turned up the radio to take my mind off everything. It barely made a dent.

My body ached with exhaustion, but more than that I ached for Adam's touch. So much so that when I turned onto my street and saw him standing outside the house, my breath caught and panic clawed at my chest. For a split second I thought I was seeing things again. But then he spoke, and I exhaled. He was real.

"Hi." He waved a solemn hand, looking a little bashful. "I hope you don't mind me just turning up."

The sight of him steadied something inside me like I'd finally reached safety. He opened his arms with that warm, familiar smile I loved so much.

"Hey, stranger," I murmured as I sank into him, letting the warmth of his embrace dissolve all of my tension. I nuzzled my nose into his chest and inhaled him deeply. "I would never mind you just turning up."

"Just wanted to check in on my favourite girl," he replied as he brushed a loose strand of hair from my face, though clearly to turn up mid-week he'd sensed how much I needed him with me. "You've been going through a lot."

I grinned as we made our way up the driveway. Everything was right in my world again. But just as we reached the front steps, Norris Bale appeared on his porch. He wore the same scowl as our previous encounter, but this time he directed it straight at Adam. The old man's eyes narrowed and his lips pursed in that same suspicious way he'd looked at me. Adam, ever polite, gave him a small nod.

"Evening, sir."

"You're back again, are you?" the man muttered, clearly unimpressed with poor Adam.

His tone was laced with something more than just irritation. Suspicion? Disdain? It was hard to tell, but it made my skin crawl. It was unusual. Everyone liked Adam. He had that charm that could win over the grumpiest of people normally.

"I'm just here helping Piper settle in." Adam's expression

stayed neutral, though I could feel the irritation simmering beneath.

The man gave a huff as he retreated inside but not before casting one last judgmental look over his shoulder. Adam waited until he was gone then sighed loudly.

"Your new neighbour is a ray of sunshine."

"Trust me, you're not the only person Norris Bale doesn't like." I rolled my eyes trying to brush off the awkwardness. "He's harmless, though. I think."

We made our way inside and Adam helped me slip off my long, puffy coat and hung it up on an empty hook for me.

"Wow, you've been busy in here," he said appreciatively as we walked into the living room.

"I have." I nodded. "It needed to be less them and more me. Look, I brought some beige paint for the living room. I'm going to do it this weekend."

"Don't keep yourself too busy. You really look tired, love. Didn't sleep well?" His fingers gripped my shoulders as he studied my face.

"Actually," I hesitated, then led him to the sofa, though we didn't sit. "I cleaned the spare room enough to sleep in, but I still didn't sleep amazingly well. I had that dream again. The one about the fire."

"I'm sorry, babe." He pulled me close, resting his chin on my head. "That sounds horrible. Was it any clearer this time?"

"Not really. Just the same faceless boy pulling me toward the fire. I keep waking up feeling like it's real, like I can feel the flames on my scars." I shook my head trying to clear the dread. "Then there was the note, which didn't help."

"Yeah, I've been thinking about that. I hate the idea of someone lurking around and leaving messages for you." Adam tensed, tightening his hold on me. "Are you sure you don't want to report it to the police?"

"I don't know." I looked over at him. Concern was etched in his eyes. I squeezed his hand. "Maybe it was nothing. My name wasn't on it. But if anything else happens, I'll call them myself. I promise."

"Good," he said, but his expression didn't relax. He brushed his thumb over the back of my hand where the scars began. "I just want you to feel safe."

I leaned into him and placed my head in the crook of his shoulder, where I fit just right. I swear his body was made for mine; he was so perfect. We stood like that for a moment, quiet but close as I listened to his heartbeat. I felt so much better being close to him I couldn't bear to let him go.

Finally, he cleared his throat and pulled me down to sit on the sofa. I could see he had more questions. My heart skipped at his expression. There was something on his mind.

"How have you been, though? Really," he asked, his voice softer. "With everything that's happened. Not just this or Evelyn but with the baby too."

A familiar ache rose in my chest, and I had to take a deep breath to steady myself. I hadn't told him I was sticking to my special diet to help us get pregnant again. I didn't want him to freak out.

"It's been hard," I admitted. "I thought I was handling it, you know, but some days it just hits me. And then with work and moving back here."

I trailed off, not sure how to explain the weight I'd been carrying. Or the aching pain I felt every time I saw a brand new little baby being pushed down the street or a proud pregnant woman simply walking around the supermarket. Adam picked up on it, though, as he always did, and rubbed my back in slow, gentle circles.

"I'm here for all of it. You know that, right? We can try again whenever you're ready. Or we can take as much time as you need. But you don't have to go through this alone. Not any of it."

"I don't want to give up, Adam. I want to try again too. It's not like we planned getting pregnant the first time, but I was so happy when we found out. I was just scared to bring it up in case. Well, I don't know. I didn't want to add more pressure."

"There's no pressure, Piper." He cupped my face gently. His thumb brushed across my cheek. "We'll take it one step at a time. I just want to be with you. But if we are planning on trying again, then maybe I should just move in. That way you don't have to face any of this alone."

"You'd really want to live here?" A smile tugged at my lips despite everything. "With the ever-charming Norris next door?"

"I'd brave a hundred grumpy old men if it means I get to come home to you."

His eyes softened as he kissed me, and the sadness in me lifted a little. Hope and belonging replaced it as I realised I really wasn't alone anymore. I had Adam, and we were moving forward together no matter what came our way. He was the person I belonged with, not whoever had written that damn note.

We stayed like that on the sofa holding each other in a comforting silence for a while. My breathing finally settled as my body loosened against his.

Then came the knock. We both froze and exchanged wary glances. The sound came from the front door.

"Are you expecting anyone?" Adam asked, his brow furrowed.

"No," I murmured, shaking my head slowly. "No one should be here."

I was suddenly even more grateful that Adam had turned up. His hand slipped from mine as he stood and moved towards the door. I got up to follow him, and a strange chill settled over me as we reached the hallway. He hesitated before pulling open the door.

No one was there. Adam stepped outside and glanced down both sides of the road. I peered over his shoulder only to see that the street was deserted. It was as still as it had been when I'd pulled up earlier. Then a faint rustling came from the bushes near the driveway. Adam froze, his eyes narrowing as he scanned the street, but nothing moved.

"Probably just kids messing around," he muttered, though he didn't sound entirely convinced.

I forced a small laugh, trying to ease the tension, but there was an odd prickling at the back of my neck. We exchanged one last look before he closed the door and locked it behind us. His hand found mine as we turned back towards the living room.

"Come on," he mumbled. "Let's just get some dinner."

I nodded and followed him to the kitchen. After we ate, we went upstairs to bed, but the strange feeling clung to me like a shadow. We undressed, and I laid there in the dark with his arms wrapped around me and his soft kisses warm against my neck. I should have felt safe. I should have felt at peace. But I couldn't shake the feeling that someone else was there watching, just beyond the edge of the light.

The Boys

The institution at night was a place of uneasy quiet. The stillness amplified the faint clink of keys from distant corridors. Shadows pooled in the corners and stretched along the dull, linoleum floors. The air carried a distinct scent that clung to the walls. It was fear maybe, or despair. Whatever it was, the darkness only made it stronger.

Two boys sat quietly in the common room, hiding from the night staff. The first was thin and small, and he lounged in a battered armchair with the stuffing poking out of its seams. He tapped a restless rhythm on the arm with his long fingers, and his sharp eyes darted toward every sound. Dark hair fell into his face, but he didn't bother to push it back.

Across the room, the second boy leaned against a table. He was taller and more solid than the first boy, and he had an air of quiet control. His gaze was steady, as though he was watching something the rest of the world couldn't see.

"You ever wonder what our families are doing out there?" the wiry boy asked, breaking the silence.

The second boy didn't move. "What they're doing? Sleeping, probably."

"Probably having fun without us," the first boy said in a low voice. "Don't you ever think about them?"

The second boy finally turned his head, though his bland expression remained unreadable.

"No. They don't want us. Why think about them?"

"Don't you want to be back out there with everyone?"

"No. There's nothing out there for people like us."

"You don't believe that." The first boy scoffed, his tapping fingers speeding up.

"No," the second boy admitted. His lips curled into a faint smile. "But it's what they want us to believe."

The wiry boy grinned back.

"I knew you were different. You're not like the other boys here. They're all nuts."

The second boy stood, his movements slow. He walked to the small window set high in the wall and peered out at the security lights beyond.

"They won't keep us here forever. We just have to pretend to be normal again."

"Yeah. They can't keep us here," the wiry boy said quickly, leaning forward. "I thought that, too."

"Not if we don't let them," the second boy replied in a calm tone. He turned back. His dark eyes glinted in the dim light. "But you have to be ready. You have to prove you can do what needs to be done."

The first boy hesitated. His grin faltered.

"What do you mean?"

"I mean," the second boy said, stepping closer, "we can't just leave. We have to send a message to everyone first not to fuck with us."

The wiry boy shifted in his seat. His fingers curled into the torn fabric of the armchair.

"What kind of message do we need to send?"

The second boy's smile widened, but it wasn't friendly.

"Follow me."

Without waiting for a response, he strode toward the door. After a moment of hesitation, the wiry boy scrambled to his feet and followed. They tiptoed through the corridors, past locked doors and a sleeping orderly until they reached the room of another boy. A smaller, younger boy who often kept to himself.

The second boy stopped outside the door with his hand resting on the handle. He turned to the wiry boy, his expression cold.

"If you want to leave with me, then show me you're serious. You have to do it."

"Do what?" The wiry boy's eyes widened.

"Scare him," the second boy said simply. "Make him understand that we're not like him. That we're in control."

"I don't know if I want to." The wiry boy hesitated, his hands trembled.

"Didn't you kill your sister?" The second boy's gaze hardened.

"Yes, but everyone got mad and locked me away in here!"

"That's exactly what happened to me, but they aren't going to control us anymore. Are they? So do as I say. Show them you're not weak. You're not going to stay here and behave silently while they have fun without us."

The wiry boy swallowed hard, his throat bobbing. Then he nodded, his movements jerky.

"Okay."

The second boy pushed the door open, and the wiry boy stepped inside. The younger kid was asleep, curled up on his narrow bed with his back to the room. The wiry boy crept closer, his heart pounding so loudly he thought it might wake the other boy up.

"Do it now," the second boy hissed from the doorway.

The wiry boy reached out. His hand shook as he grabbed the blanket and yanked it away. The younger boy woke with a start, his eyes wide with fear. Before he could scream, the wiry boy clamped a hand over his mouth.

And tightened one over his throat.

The younger boy thrashed, his muffled cries lost in the heavy silence of the room. His small hands clawed at the wiry boy's arms, nails scraping against skin.

A floorboard creaked. The second boy stepped forward.

"That's enough," he said as he stepped over to the bed. He leaned down, his face inches from the younger boy's. "You're going to forget this ever happened. Understand?"

The younger boy nodded frantically. Tears streamed down his face. The second boy straightened, his gaze flicking to the wiry boy.

"See? That wasn't so hard. Well done."

The wiry boy let go of the boy's mouth and stumbled backwards. The second boy clapped him on the shoulder, his grip firm.

"You did good. But next time, you'll have to do more."

As they slipped back into the shadows, the wiry boy's hands wouldn't stop shaking. But the second boy didn't even blink. He showed no fear. No hesitation; only triumph.

Piper

I woke early Wednesday morning after sleeping properly for the first time since last week. Though it was too dark to see Adam's face, I could feel his arm draped across my waist, keeping me safe even in sleep. I'd dated before; one guy even lasted two years. But I'd never felt a love like I felt for Adam. He was just the right amount of caring, protective, and sexy. He yawned and a sense of calm settled over my chest. His eyes slowly opened, and he smiled.

"Good morning, beautiful," he murmured, his voice thick with sleep as he pulled me closer.

"Good morning," I replied with a smile.

The call of work pulled at the back of my mind but I pushed it away as I nestled into his chest and let the rest of the world fade away for a while. His fingers trailed over my bare back and down to my thighs as he gently pushed me onto my back and kissed me. He was soft at first, but it turned into a deep kiss that made me feel like I was his oxygen.

I watched him dress after we made love, too at peace to move. I even loved the way he pulled on his clothes and adjusted his collar in the mirror. Every little movement he did was fascinating to me.

"I wish I didn't have to run." He turned to me with his brow slightly creased. "Got a new patient at nine, and traffic back to Harrogate's going to be a nightmare at this time."

I nodded and wrapped my naked body in the bedcovers as I perched on the edge of the mattress and tried to quickly sort out my knotted hair.

"I'll miss you," I told him, trying to hide how sad I really was at him leaving.

"Hey, I'll be back before you know it," he said, flashing me that affable grin that always made me feel better. "And it's not like we haven't got all the time in the world. We've got plans, remember?"

"Yes," I said, grinning despite myself as he waggled his eyebrows in a manner he must have thought was suggestive.

I waved from the bedroom window as he drove away. The house suddenly felt far too still without his presence. I forced myself to shower and get dressed, then gathered up my work things and headed out.

The morning air was fresh. It lifted my spirits as I climbed into the car. I've always loved winter. Too much sun wasn't for me. My pale skin couldn't handle it. And this year would be a new start for both of us. I had a new sense of purpose. I was going to create my own family with Adam. It was everything I'd ever wanted.

I hummed under my breath as I moved through the hallways of Pinevale. The weight that had pressed on my chest since moving back felt lighter today, as if Adam's visit had somehow taken it with him. I greeted Margaret with a bright smile, and to my surprise, the older woman's expression showed actual recognition.

"Good morning, Margaret!" I said.

I gently guided her away from the filing cabinet she'd been

opening and closing repeatedly. She blinked and glanced up at me.

"Oh. You're the new one?" she asked, her brows knitting together.

"Yep. It's me," I replied with a warm smile.

I moved through to the kitchen and helped Sue restock the fridge with the freshly delivered shopping. Sue watched me carefully out of the corner of her eye, but she was definitely more at ease around me than she had been the past couple of days.

"Hey, Piper. How are you doing?"

"Not bad, thanks."

"Good. Keep an eye on Margaret today. She seems to be getting worse. She rang the pizza place six times last night in thirty minutes because she couldn't remember if she's already ordered."

She grinned and I had to hold back a sympathetic laugh. Poor Margaret. Poor pizza place.

"I'll keep an eye on her. Have you got much planned for your day off tomorrow?" I asked, slotting eggs into the fridge rack.

"Maybe a quiet one this time." Sue gave a small nod. Her gaze rested on me. "You seem in better spirits today."

"Yeah, I suppose I am." I felt myself blush. "Sorry if I've seemed off. I'm still finding my feet with all the upheaval."

Sue gave me a brief, approving nod and then turned back to her tasks. Her smile faded into a focused expression. I didn't mind. She would never replace Evelyn, but it felt like we were making progress with each other after the rocky start on Monday.

During lunch, I met a couple of the other patients. There was Aidan, a twenty-seven-year-old man with pale skin and a shaved head who'd lost his mind after taking too many drugs. I hadn't read his file yet, but he seemed well and would probably be ready to live on his own soon.

Then Rosie, who was barely sixteen and fresh out of the local psych ward. She suffered from delusions, but during lunch she was a sweet, smiley kid who I would've guessed was only about fourteen.

The last patient was Gregg, a stoney faced guy who didn't say a word or even look at me. I hadn't got around to reading his file, so I didn't know why he needed to be in assisted living. Then Peter entered the room, and the atmosphere changed. He grinned widely at everyone, and little Rosie was the only one who grinned back.

"You must be Piper," he said as he pulled my palm into a handshake. "Nice to meet you properly."

"Nice to meet you too, Peter," I replied warmly, despite my internal warning system buzzing like a live wire. I was experienced enough to tell a dangerous patient pretty quickly when I saw one. His grip was firm, but it stayed a second too long. His eyes flicked over my face as if he were sizing me up. I'd met his type plenty of times before. He was charming, but dangerous, and excellent at lying and manipulating.

"Settling in okay, are we?" he asked.

"Yes, thank you." I forced myself to hold his gaze.

"It's nice seeing someone new here." His lips quirked into a half-smile.

There was a humour in his eyes that caught me off guard, though I didn't show it.

"Thank you, Peter," I said.

I kept my voice even as I moved on, though my pulse was a little quicker than before. There was something unnerving in his charm, and yet he was nothing like the guarded person who had stared me down the other day outside of his apartment.

He ate lunch jovially with the other patients, but Margaret stayed well away from him, and Lily cast nervous glances his way as she pretended to eat a bowl of soup. I felt a stab of protectiveness at the idea of him upsetting Lily. She reminded me so much of myself at her age.

By the end of my shift, though, I felt lighter. The day had gone well, and the clients were being friendly towards me. It was different to the psych ward, where the patients mistrusted us and were still severely ill. Those patients were often severely paranoid or in the middle of a psychotic break. But things at Pinevale House might just be fine. Especially when Adam moved here. I hoped he wouldn't take too long. I felt happier than I had all week as I left work and looked forward to dinner.

But as I walked to my car, I saw it. There was another flash of white tucked under the wiper blade. My heart sank, and the now familiar chill of being watched spread across my skin. I hesitated as I approached the car. The empty car park suddenly felt far too open and quiet. My hand hovered for a moment before I reached for the note. The rough edge of the paper caught against my fingers as I unfolded it.

And there it was again, the same cramped handwriting as before. Except this time, the author had addressed it directly to me.

The Shadow

Dear Piper,

It's strange, isn't it? How quickly you settle back into old places as if you never left. You fit right back in, though you seem a little different now. Softer, maybe. More trusting. But don't worry, I'm here to look out for you.

I've been watching, you know. You're making yourself at home, picking up little routines, making all the right gestures at work.

Do you feel at ease? It must be comforting, finding something familiar again.

But sometimes I notice the way you glance over your shoulder, a quick little glance of the eyes like you're searching for something. Or someone.

Are you afraid? Or maybe just being careful? It's good to be cautious, Piper. We can't have you taking any risks, can we?

But the people you're getting close to are stepping in places they shouldn't. Not everyone suits your side. Some people just don't belong there. I don't think they really see you, not in the way they should.

I do, though. And I'll make sure no one gets too close. Don't worry, I'll always be here, right behind you, monitoring things.

You don't remember yet, but I've taken care over the years

to understand what you need. I know what keeps you steady. I see the things that could threaten you, and I can deal with those.

You've had enough upheaval. A fresh start is important, but we can't just let anyone waltz into your life without paying attention.

Work is a comfort, isn't it? But be careful who you trust there. Not everyone deserves your kindness. There's one who stays too close. Watch them, Piper. They don't belong in your life, and I won't let them stay.

So keep going, Piper. Settle in, do your work, smile. You deserve to be happy and you're trying so hard, but you don't have to do this alone. You never have because you've always had me.

Just remember, I'm here to make sure you don't lose yourself. I'll make sure of it. After all, we wouldn't want you to get hurt again.

You don't need to worry, Piper. I'll make sure they stay away. I've always known what's best for you, haven't I?

You'll see.

Piper

My hands trembled as I stared down at the note. The words twisted my stomach and shattered the brief calm I'd been enjoying. I scanned the empty car park and my eyes darted to the shadows that stretched across the pavement. Was the author hiding in one of those shadows watching me, waiting to see my reaction?

I remembered Lily's face peering at me the other night and glanced back at the house. There were no faces this time. I looked back down at the note as if maybe it had disappeared. The words pulsed on the page. Swallowing hard, I clutched it tighter as a wave of dread washed over me. It was quickly followed by a sudden loneliness.

I needed to talk to someone. Someone who might make sense of it, and Sue was the only person nearby. I turned and rushed back inside. She was in the staff room, stacking files.

"Sue!" My voice came out sharper than I intended. She looked up, her brows lifting in surprise.

"What's wrong?" she asked as she set down a folder. "I thought you'd gone home."

"Someone left another one on my car." I held up the note. "Someone's watching me. They wrote my name this time. Maybe it was Peter."

I swallowed, trying to steady myself. Sue's eyes narrowed as she read the note. For a second, she looked almost uncomfortable or guilty. But just as quickly, her usual calm mask slipped back into place.

"Piper, these sorts of things happen all the time," she said with a sigh. "And I can tell you right now, this isn't Peter or any of the other patients. People don't like living near places like this. They hear 'mentally ill' and assume the worst. Some of them would love nothing more than to stir up trouble and get us shut down. They could be trying to get a reaction out of you. And are you sure it's not just someone you know messing around? You've had a stressful month with a big move and a new job. Maybe you're reading into this more than you need to."

"So you think there's nothing to worry about?" I frowned. "That I'm overreacting?"

"No, that's not what I mean. I just think you've got a lot on your plate right now," she replied as her gaze moved to the window.

"What are you looking at?" I asked. My pulse quickened. I followed her gaze. "Did you see someone?"

"No! Jeez, Piper," she huffed, shaking her head. "I just thought I saw something move, that's all."

I followed her gaze, my stomach twisting, but there was nothing outside other than a quiet street and the wind stirring the bare branches outside.

"I'm just saying if a daft letter has got you feeling this way, maybe a little distance would help. Take a day or two. Get your head clear. It's probably nothing, but sometimes space helps put things into perspective."

I clenched the note so tightly it crumpled in my hand.

"Right. Thanks for the advice," I muttered, my voice tight.

I stalked out of the staff room. Her scepticism was still biting at me as I stepped outside into the cold again. The sting of it made me shiver, or maybe that was just the regret settling in my chest. I'd stormed off, but now I was alone in the dark car park again.

I really needed to pull myself together.

I scanned the car park. Everything looked the same as it had when I arrived, but somehow it felt different. I rushed to my car, fumbling with the keys as I unlocked the door and slipped inside. The moment the lock clicked, I exhaled and pressed my back against the seat.

Then pulled out my phone and dialled Adam's number.

"Hey, Piper," he answered. His voice was so warm and familiar it instantly made me feel better.

"Adam," I said, my voice still tight. "It happened again. I got another note. But this one feels different. I think they're watching me. They mentioned someone being close to me, and I think they're threatening you. I don't know what to do."

Adam was silent for a moment. I bit my lip praying I hadn't scared him off. He dealt with unstable people all day at work. He didn't need me adding to it.

"Are you sure they were threatening someone?"

"Yes, Adam! And Sue just made me feel like I was imagining it but she saw the letter. She's given me a couple of days off work like I'm some kind of paranoid wreck. I think it's because I mentioned Peter might be responsible but there's definitely something off about him."

"Peter who?"

"Shit! I'm not supposed to name patients. Forget I said that."

"Look, if it's scaring you, call the police. Maybe they can help. You shouldn't have to deal with this on your own."

"Okay. I'll do that." I took a shaky breath and nodded to myself.

"Don't put it off. Hang up and call them now. Let me know what they say."

"Yes, babe. I'll do it now."

My hands were still trembling as I dialled the police station, and the phone rang out for some time. When they finally picked up I was a whole ball of nerves.

"How can I help?" The woman asked in a warm voice. She sounded nice at least, so I explained what had happened about the notes.

"I thought the first note might have been a patient in my new job, but now I'm not so sure."

"Where are you now, miss?"

"I'm in my car. Right outside work in the car park of Pinevale House."

"Do you feel threatened or endangered right now?"

"Erm." I looked around the dark street. A chill creeped into my spine despite their emptiness.

"Not particularly, I guess."

"Okay. Go home. I've made the incident report. We'll get back to you within a few days, Miss Roberts. If you see any suspicious behaviour or feel directly threatened, then call us immediately."

"A few days?" I repeated, my voice rising with frustration. "Someone's threatening me! How am I supposed to feel safe?"

"We have your details. Someone will be in touch soon. I'd suggest staying with a friend."

She hung up before I could argue. I sat there with the words "a few days" ringing in my ears. A surge of anger simmered beneath my fear. How could they take this so lightly?

I drove home still fuming, glancing out of the rearview mirror every few seconds. My paranoia was seeping into every movement I saw. The words echoed in my head, making me question everyone I'd spoken to today. By the time I reached the house, the adrenaline was wearing off and I was exhausted.

A couple of hours later as I was numbly stirring a cup of tea on the sofa, my phone rang. The screen displayed an unknown number and my heart skipped a beat. I hesitated, then answered cautiously.

"Piper?" a calm, deep voice came through the line. "This is Detective Inspector Alex Swanson. I understand you're dealing with an unsettling situation. I'd like to come by in the morning to have a chat and see if there's anything we can do. Will you be available around eight a.m.?"

"Yes, yes, absolutely. Thank you." Relief washed over me. "Thank you for coming over so quickly."

"Not a problem. Try to get some rest," he said. His tone was so reassuring, like he might really be able to help me. "I'll see you then."

As I hung up, hope broke through my fear. Maybe this Detective Swanson could finally make sense of it all. Maybe, I'd finally get some answers.

Piper

The dream was sharper that night, as if I was closer than ever to understanding what it meant.

Or maybe that just meant I was losing my mind again.

Flames roared around me like a searing wall that stretched high and wide. Smoke turned the air thick, and it was almost too hot to breathe. And just beyond the fire was the boy. The one I loved so much I would walk into the fire for.

He stood with his back to me and his small shoulders hunched. The heat from the flames made his shape bend. I reached out and called to him like I had done many times before. He never faced me.

Until now.

He turned, moving slowly as the flames half-lit up his face. His features were blurred but almost recognisable. Just a little closer and I'd finally know who he was. My heart raced as the fire rushed around us.

Just as I thought I might finally see his face, he vanished. The bright flames that surged up swallowed his body, cutting off his shape completely before they came for me too.

I woke up with a jolt.

My chest was tight and heaving and my fingers curled around

the sheets as I tried to bring myself back to the here and now.

It was just a dream

But it didn't feel that way. I could still feel the sear of the heat and smell the smoke, and my wrists ached. I gripped my wrist and rubbed the old scars. They were hot under my touch.

The clock read seven thirty a.m., and my stomach twisted as I realised I'd overslept. It was Thursday, and Alex Swanson was supposed to be here at eight a.m.. I needed to pull myself together before then. If he turned up to interview a trembling mess with burning scars then he would never take my concerns about the note seriously. Nobody would.

I forced my tired body out of the spare bedroom and into the creaky bathroom, standing under the cold spray of the shower until my heartbeat steadied and I could think straight once more. Then I quickly got dried and dressed in jeans and a casual jumper.

I moved slower than usual as the edges of the dream clung to me and refused to fully let go. Even after waking up, the smoke stung my nostrils and the boy's image lingered. It was etched into the back of my eyelids. My chest ached. Not just from fear but from the unbearable yearning to know who he was and why I felt like I'd lost him a thousand times before.

When the knock came at the door at eight a.m. sharp, I was ready. Or as ready as I could be. I took a breath and pulled the door open to face Detective Alex Swanson. He was tall and broad, with a chest that seemed to fill the doorway and a thick, dark beard.

He wore a cheap, black suit that hadn't been ironed well. I imagined he'd be more comfortable wearing outdoor sportswear. Maybe for rugby. His expression was gruff, almost intimidating, but there was warmth in his eyes. Or maybe that was my wishful thinking.

"Piper Roberts," he greeted me in a low voice and stuck out his enormous hand. I offered mine. His palm was cool from the cold air, and our handshake was firm but brief. "Thanks for letting me come by."

"Of course," I replied, stepping back and letting him into the house after he flashed his ID. "Thank you for coming."

His gaze drifted over the hallway, taking everything in through sharp eyes as he made his way to the dining table in the centre of the kitchen. I'd done my best to tidy up, but the place suddenly felt cramped, like his imposing presence filled up all the space. I sat down at the table, and he took a seat across from me. His hands rested on his notebook as he opened it up.

"Would you like a drink?" I asked.

"No, thank you. I understand you've been receiving unsettling letters outside of your place of work?" he asked, looking at me closely. Talk about getting straight to business. "Do you mind if I have a look at them?"

I nodded and grabbed my black handbag from the kitchen counter to retrieve the two letters.

"Yes, that;s right. The first one didn't have my name on it so I wasn't sure if it was for me, but they used my name in the second one. Hang on, sorry I can't feel them."

I stopped talking as I looked down to search the handbag, but it was no use. Panic built as I realised there was no paper in my handbag. The letters were gone.

I dug my hand deeper into the bag, my face creased in confusion.

"They were right here," I mumbled, almost to myself. I glanced up and DI Swanson raised an eyebrow. "Sorry about this. Let me just check the bedroom. I have been worrying all night, so maybe I moved them somewhere and forgot."

I left him in the kitchen, ran upstairs and ransacked the spare room and the bathroom. The letters were nowhere to be found. A lump formed in my throat but I swallowed it back down. He'd never believe I was sane if I lost it. I strode back into the kitchen, though my legs were shaky as hell.

"I can't find them. I don't understand."

"Maybe you accidentally binned them?" DI Swanson suggested.

"No! I wouldn't have. Someone must have taken them."

"From your handbag?" he asked.

"From the house! They must know where I live. They must have got in here somehow." I could hear my voice rising in panic and although I wanted to stay calm, I was becoming more out of control with each word.

"It's unsettling, no doubt," he said, his voice much calmer than mine. "Let's take a moment to think about where they could be."

"It's more than unsettling!"

How could he stay so composed when my world felt like it was falling apart?

"Take a seat, Piper. It will be okay. Let's work through this together. You work at Pinevale House, yes?"

"Yes, I do. Just started on Monday." I nodded, feeling a bit thrown by the shift in conversation. I took a seat. "This is my parents' house. I moved in last week from Harrogate."

Swanson's gaze drifted down to my wrists, where the scars were visible. He said nothing. I hastily pulled the sleeves of my jumper over my wrists.

"Oh? Where are your parents if not here?"

"Dead."

The word sounded heartless, and I rushed to explain further.

"It wasn't recent. They died three years ago."

"And you've only just moved in here?"

"Yes, after my boss died two months ago." Shit. I really needed to stop spilling my life story to this man. He didn't need to know everything.

"Wow. That's a lot to go through. I bet you needed a fresh start, eh?"

"I suppose." I shrugged.

"Are you doing alright in the new job?"

"What do you mean?"

"Are you doing okay with it after the deaths and the move? I mean, anyone would struggle in your situation. Are you well supported?"

"I'm fine," I replied, a little too quickly. Hopefully he couldn't hear the edge in my voice. "I worked in a secure psychiatric hospital in Harrogate so I'm used to threats. I'm not easily rattled. But this is different. My mental health isn't the issue here. I just need whoever's doing this to stop."

"I understand." He nodded slowly, eyes narrowing as he watched me. "Sometimes these situations bring up old stuff for people. It's a normal reaction."

His voice was gentle, like he was trying to reach past whatever defences I had up, but his words reminded me of conversations I'd had with therapists long ago.

I wasn't interested in going down that road again.

"I appreciate the concern but I'm fine. This person is the issue, not me. You need to speak to the patients. I'm allowed to tell you their names because you're with the police, right? I think Peter might know something, or Lily. She's always

105

watching him."

There was a pause as he held my gaze, and I felt myself bristling, wanting him to understand that I didn't need him to coddle me or handle the situation delicately. I just needed answers. He seemed to sense it, nodding once, and closed his notebook.

"These things can take time," he said finally, standing to leave. "Especially when interviewing people in sensitive settings like a mental health facility. There are permissions to get and protocols to follow. But I have a colleague who can help. I'll keep you updated."

"Right." I clenched my jaw, my frustration rising again. That was it?

"Do you feel safe here? Maybe staying with a friend for a couple of nights would be a good idea."

"No." I can't tell him I don't have any friends left here. I didn't have any before I left, really. Then he'd know I was pathetic. "I'll ask my boyfriend to come round."

"Great."

Swanson reached for his notebook, flipping a few pages. His expression shifted slightly, like he was weighing whether to say something. Finally, he glanced up.

"Before I go, do you know Hayley Smith?"

"The name doesn't ring a bell."

He gave me one last look. That same warmth once again broke through his otherwise serious expression.

"Look, Piper, we'll monitor this. But call me if you need anything." He paused, giving me a card with his number on it. "We'll figure it out."

With that, he turned and headed for the door. I closed the door behind him and rested my forehead against it as I let out a shaky breath. I forced myself to move to the living room.

I caught my reflection in the window as I straightened the cushions on the sofa. My face was pale, and my eyes were hollowed by too many restless nights. Whoever this person was, they had a grip on my life I needed to shake.

I wasn't sure if I'd get the answers I wanted from Alex Swanson. It was worth a shot, but I had to look into this myself too. Someone had been in my house. They'd been close enough to touch my things. Close enough to know exactly where I'd kept the letters. They hadn't just left me with no evidence. They'd made it clear how easily they could get to me.

They could be watching me right now.

I pulled out my phone and typed a quick message to Sue.

"Sorry about yesterday. I was being silly. I'm feeling much better. I'll be coming in today."

Going back to work might not be the right choice, but staying at the house and stewing in my own thoughts wasn't an option. I needed to do something, anything, to keep moving. And if there was one place I knew this person spent time, it was Pinevale House.

Swanson

The station was quieter than usual as most officers were still out in the field looking for Hayley Smith. DCI Murray had completed the press release so Hayley's disappearance was now public knowledge. The public had set up a search group for clues near her last known address. People were heartbroken by the story of a caring, pretty woman who had no friends or family and apparently a made-up boyfriend for all they could tell.

Swanson leaned against the edge of his desk with his arms folded in his brand-new office. Murray had finally allowed him his own small area. She didn't say it in as many words, but he knew it was a thank you for keeping her and Hart's relationship a secret. Not that he needed a gift to keep quiet. What they did outside of work was their business. Office politics were not of any interest to him.

The office wasn't much bigger than the cupboard he used to hide in, but it was officially his at least. Although Summer and Hart didn't seem to have got the message.

Summer perched on a chair across from him. Her hands rested on her bump. He wished she'd go home where it was safer. She'd been dragged into this whole thing by Perry's phone call. Why was he going round calling Summer and handing him and Hart notes if he didn't want to talk?

Hart sprawled on the worn office chair in the corner. Her boot tapped against the floor as she read something on her phone.

"I went to see someone this morning," Swanson said. He thought back to scared Piper and how she'd reminded him of the first time he met Summer, who'd been going through something similar when her case ended up in his lap.

"That's nice," Hart quipped, not looking up from the screen. "Watch out, Summer."

Summer smirked, shaking her head. Swanson didn't even acknowledge Hart's comment and kept speaking.

"Her name's Piper Roberts. She's been getting unsolicited letters left on her car. Real strange ones." He tapped a folder on his desk. "She's scared. Thinks someone's been in her house because the letters suddenly disappeared when she went to show them to me. She's also a mental health worker just like Hayley Smith."

That got Hart's attention like he knew it would. It was the reason he'd taken on Piper's complaint.

"What kind of letters?" Hart straightened, pocketing her phone.

"Handwritten creepy ones saying they're watching her and those around her. Whoever's writing them signs off with the same phrase every time *"You'll see"*. She has no idea who it might be."

"Charming." Hart gave a low whistle. "So what's her story?"

"She just moved back into her parents' house from Harrogate. Said she's had a rough few years. Her parents died a while back. I looked into it, and they were that couple who were shot by the mentally ill guy three years ago, which she didn't mention."

"Wow! Michael something?" Summer asked.

"Yep. Michael Grey."

"Jeez." Hart whistled through her teeth. "We worked on that case the year before we met you, Summer. Not that there was much to work on. He admitted to everything. Multiple CCTV cameras caught him. He just walked down Cathedral Street shooting people. He killed a couple holding hands, and injured a few others. There was that bloke who got shot in the leg, and the little girl who got caught on the arm. Thank god she survived at least."

"So that couple he shot dead were Piper's parents?" Summer asked, looking at Swanson.

"Yep. It's weird she didn't mention it. It's a big thing to go through. That alone could cause a hell of a lot of stress. It was three years ago, and she said she's only just moved into their house so it must have affected her pretty badly. She hasn't even cleared it out yet, there's stuff all over the place."

"Jeez. Poor woman," Summer muttered sadly.

"That's not all of it. She used to work in a psychiatric unit in Harrogate, but she also lost her boss recently. When I googled it, I found out a manager of a psychiatric hospital in Harrogate was shot two months ago. It must be her."

"That's dodgy," Hart quipped.

"These strange letters apparently started on day one of her new job," Swanson continued. "She started working at Pinevale House on Monday, so it's nowhere near the one Hayley worked in. Oakleigh is in Ilkeston. She mentioned the possibility the letters could be connected to someone she's interacted with at the home, but she doesn't know who. Gave me a couple of possible names to look into."

"And you believe her even though she's gone through all of that, and these letters have disappeared?" Hart tilted her head, her brow furrowed.

"Yes, I think I do. She was shaken up but not erratic. Even when she couldn't find the letters. She swore they were in her bag. She thinks whoever's been writing them got into the house and took them."

"She sounds paranoid to me," Hart said, crossing her arms. "I think she needs Summer more than she needs us."

"Maybe." Swanson met her gaze. "But if you'd seen the look in her eyes, you'd think twice. Something's off here, and I want to dig into it before we dismiss her outright. We've had one mental health worker disappear already."

"You said she works at which mental health home?" Summer shifted in her seat.

"Pinevale House." Swanson shifted in his chair. "I want to check the place out in case there's any link to the Hayley Smith disappearance. Maybe someone is targeting health care workers or maybe it's a patient who has stayed at both homes and knows them both. Some patients have a history of violent or stalking behaviour, but it's not like we can just walk in there and start asking questions. That's where you come in."

"You want me to help interview people?" Summer asked.

"Not right away," Swanson replied "I need to get the permissions sorted first and make sure everything's done by the book. But when the time comes, you've got the training to navigate those conversations in a way that won't spook anyone."

"Well, that didn't work with Perry Vance. Am I the only one wondering if this is a dead end?" Hart raised a hand. "I mean, what if this is all just in her head? No offense, but she's been through three murders and the whole 'missing letters' thing doesn't exactly scream credible."

"Maybe." Swanson's jaw tightened. "But what if it's not? I'm not writing her off until I know more."

"Fair enough." Hart shrugged. "I just hope she's not spinning a story knowing Hayley is missing. We've seen it happen before."

"It's worth checking out. I know what it's like to have strange things happen and have no one believe you." Summer shot Hart a disapproving look before turning back to Swanson. "So I'll help. But if she's this scared, have you thought about asking her to stay somewhere else? Just until we know more."

"She didn't seem too keen on leaving," Swanson admitted. "I'm not sure she has anywhere to go. But I'll bring it up again next time I see her."

"What gets me is why they disappeared? Wouldn't a stalker want her to have them?" Summer asked.

"Good point," Swanson muttered. "So why would someone take them?"

"Unless it's about control. Or memory. If someone wants her to doubt herself, they're doing a good job."

"Well," Hart sighed and stood. "Keep me posted. But I'm betting it's someone trying to get in her head. Old school friend. Ex-lover, pissed-off neighbour, something boring like that."

Swanson didn't answer. His gut told him it was more than that. There was a connection here even if they couldn't see it yet. Piper's haunted eyes lingered in his mind, the way she'd searched for those missing letters as if her life depended on it. As Hart sauntered out, Summer stayed behind, her hand brushing his arm.

"Are you alright?" she asked gently.

"Yeah." He hesitated. "Just got a bad feeling about this one."

Summer nodded. "Then trust it."

She squeezed his arm, and he gave her a faint smile before returning to the file on his desk. Piper's story made little sense yet. But if there was one thing Swanson had learned, it was that bad feelings usually meant there was something worse waiting to be uncovered.

Piper

I stared at my phone for longer than I'd care to admit, thumb hovering over Adam's name in my call log. My stomach churned, and my mind raced through what I was about to tell him. The police can't do much. The letters are gone. Someone might've been inside my house.

He won't be happy. He might even freak out and leave me to deal with it alone, and I wouldn't blame him. But the thought of hearing his voice steadied me enough to press the button. He picked up on the second ring.

"Hi, Piper. Everything alright?"

"Yeah. No." I sniffed. "I don't know."

"Talk to me." His voice was soft, but there was a protective edge to it.

"Someone from the police station came round to the house this morning." I began pacing the kitchen as I spoke. The old wooden floor creaked under my feet. "Said he was some sort of detective. He was nice. His name was Alex Swanson. But they can't do much yet. He says they need permission to talk to anyone at the home. The patients, I mean."

I was rambling, but I couldn't stop talking long enough for my brain to form a coherent sentence.

"Permissions?" Adam sounded mildly annoyed. "You're

telling me they can't even investigate properly without red tape?"

"He said they're working on it," I blurted, trying to get to the worst bit. I stopped pacing and gripped the edge of the counter. "But, um, there's something else about the letters. They're gone."

"Gone?" Adam's tone sharpened. "What do you mean, gone? Did the detective take them?"

"No. I don't know what happened." My voice wavered. "I thought I had them in my bag, but when I went to show DI Swanson, they weren't there. I searched every room in the house, Adam. Someone must have taken them."

The words felt ridiculous as they left my mouth, but I knew deep down that's what had happened. The only alternative was that I'd lost my mind again, and that thought chilled me more than the idea of an intruder.

"Jesus, Piper." Adam exhaled slowly. "Are you sure?"

"Yes. I'm sure."

"Is it the patient you mentioned who was creeping you out? What was his name? Paul?"

"Peter? I don't know. Why would he go this far if it was a prank on someone he barely knows? I told Sue I'd go to work soon because I didn't want to stay here alone all day, but I can't think straight. I feel like I'm losing my mind again."

"You're not losing your mind." His voice was firm. "And you don't need to be alone. I'll come stay with you."

"What?" I froze mid-step and leant against the kitchen counter.

"I'll move in with you now," he said, like it was the most obvious thing in the world. "You shouldn't be dealing with this alone, and if someone is following you then it's not safe."

"What about your patients?" I asked, though part of me was already clinging to the idea of him living here in the house with me, making it feel less empty and terrifying.

"They'll manage. The staff can cover for me for a few days, and I'll talk to Sharon about taking a step back sooner rather than later. I'll need today to sort some bits so maybe go to work just for the day so you're around others and safe."

"You'd really do that?" I blinked fresh tears away as I tried to process his words.

"Of course I would." He hesitated, then said quietly, "I love you, Piper."

"I love you too," I whispered.

"And I can't wait to live with you."

"You mean it?" I asked. I had to make sure I wasn't hearing things.

"Yes. Yes, I mean it." I heard his smile in his voice. "It's settled. I'll pack a bag and head over tomorrow."

"Thank you, Adam," I replied, feeling like I could breathe again.

"Don't thank me. Just promise me you'll lock every door and window tonight, and call me if anything feels off."

"I will," I promised.

When I hung up the house was just as quiet and empty as before, but the silence suddenly didn't feel so bad. I stayed in the kitchen for a few minutes after the call as Adam's words settled over me. I could still feel the faint buzz of excitement as I got ready for work, and my hands were finally steady. *Adam* was going to live with me. No man had ever loved me enough to want to move in with me.

I pulled my hair into a loose braid, added a touch of mascara, and even caught myself humming while lacing up my boots.

The drive to the office felt lighter too. The sky was overcast and the streets were damp from the previous night's rain, but it didn't matter. Adam was coming to live with me, and we'd be safe together. He'd make sure I didn't lose my mind.

When I walked through the door of Pinevale House, I made my way straight to the communal office and greeted a couple of colleagues as I passed. Sitting down at the empty desk, I glanced at the schedule for the day on the wall. A trip out to the library in an hour, then lunch, followed by a trip to the supermarket. Busy, but manageable.

If I stayed behind, then there would be plenty of time for me to do some snooping. There was something here that could help point me towards answers, and I finally felt ready to find them.

Piper

Both Peter and Lily were out for most of the day, and my snooping around in patient files revealed no clues at all. No one had a history of leaving creepy notes from what I could see, or even teasing the staff.

Except for Peter, the rapist who had a habit of scaring patients and younger members of staff by staring at them through the dark windows late at night. Clearly he was not as ready to live in the community as the psychiatrist would have anyone believe. But there was nothing in his file about leaving people threatening letters.

By the time I got home just as the sun dipped, tired and frustrated, the house was the sort of quiet that made it feel too big. It wouldn't feel like this forever, though. Adam would be here soon, and this place would finally feel alive again. Our home, and with our baby too one day soon. But not until I dealt with the mess my parents had left behind.

Their bedroom was the only one big enough to be ours but currently it was still a shrine to them. I'd left it untouched, and it looked frozen in time. I'd avoided it for so long but tonight I had my new sense of determination to make everything perfect, and I was ready to tackle it. Plus, it would keep my hands and mind busy and stop me worrying about those damn letters.

I kicked off my boots at the bottom of the stairs, rolled up my sleeves, and headed up to the room. The air was still stale on the landing. Apart from running up to my new bedroom each night to sleep and take a quick shower, I'd barely spent any time upstairs. I definitely needed to open another window up there. The door to their bedroom groaned when I pushed it open, as if even it was reluctant to let me inside.

The sight of the bed made me pause. Their duvet was still the same awful floral thing I remembered them using when I last slept here during a rare visit, and then there were the neatly smoothed over pillows that no one had touched in years. The creepy photo still lay on the bedside table, which I ignored. A cabinet by the window sagged under random trinkets, and the wardrobe doors hung slightly ajar with clothes peeking out.

Adam wasn't there physically, but that evening was the start of our new lives together.

I made a plan to go through one drawer at a time, but I started with the cabinet first. Its bottom half was a cupboard, while the top half featured bowed shelves. I could tell it was ancient. Its paint was chipped at the edges, and the wood beneath had worn smooth in places. They had stuffed the first layer with random bits and pieces. There was a tangle of keys, old receipts faded to near-blankness, and stray buttons long forgotten about. None of it had any use, and I threw it in the black rubbish bag I'd brought upstairs.

The second layer was worse. It was crammed with old newspapers, a half-used box of birthday candles, and a photo album so water-damaged the pictures were stuck together. I couldn't even look at them. The firemen who put out the fire must have damaged it with their hoses. Maybe Dad had saved a couple of photos from it over the years, and that's why I looked younger in the photo downstairs.

Again I tossed all of it into a black bin bag and moved on. There was nothing from my parents that I really wanted to keep. I had to be ruthless if I wanted to get this place half decent.

I was about to close the door when I noticed the corner of the bottom floor of the cabinet was sticking up. I pulled at it. Maybe I could fix it and sell the cabinet to pay off some debt. I needed it gone before Adam found out how bad it was. He'd never want to live with me otherwise. When I gave it a harder tug, it came free with a sharp jerk, and revealed a whole compartment.

My brow furrowed as I looked inside the gap. It was mostly pieces of paper. Some were folded into crisp rectangles, and others had crumpled and bent at the edges. As I gathered them, I noticed they weren't random scraps of paper like the others. These were envelopes, all addressed to Jane Roberts. *Mum.*

Something cold settled in my chest. Why would my mum have kept a hidden compartment full of letters? I glanced at the top one. They were so old the ink had smudged in places. These were private, and I should not read my mother's private letters.

I carefully set them aside on the bed to work out what to do with them later. Then I worked through the rest of the mess in the cabinet quickly, dumping what I didn't need into the bin bag. But as hard as I tried I couldn't ignore the letters.

Still sitting cross-legged on the floor, I picked up the top one again. They might be important. I could just look at one to check. The envelope was brittle, and the corners curled with age. The handwriting on the front was smudged, but I could tell it was sharp and angular.

To Jane.

I opened it carefully so as to not tear the aged paper. The one-page letter inside was short. The ink had faded but still readable, though I didn't make it past the first couple of lines. I wasn't ready for the words yet.

Not when my focus was entirely on the shape of the letters themselves. Something about them itched at my memory. A wrongness that was familiar but just out of reach. It was the way the loops curled too tightly and the slant that seemed almost angry.

My breath quickened. I reached for another letter with trembling hands, and then another. Then I spread the top few out on the bed. My pulse climbed as I realised I was definitely correct.

The distinctive handwriting was the same as the notes left on my car.

The Shadow

My love,

It's strange how one night can change everything. I never thought I'd have to put this into words, but I need you to know I didn't have a choice. You've always been my world. Everything I've done has been for you and Piper. I hope one day you'll understand that.

I know you think you had to send me away. I understand I scared you. That night wasn't supposed to happen the way it did. I lost control, and I'll carry that forever. He came at you, didn't he? I saw the hatred in his eyes, and the way he towered over you like he'd won. I couldn't let him hurt you. There was no way I could let him take anything else from us. So I stepped in.

Do you remember how quiet it got after? Like the entire world had stopped to take a breath. I can still hear the thud, the way he crumpled, and the silence that followed. Piper was still in her bedroom, so it was just us in that room standing over him. She never needs to know. You said nothing. You didn't have to. Your eyes told me everything. That you loved me enough that we'd never speak of it again.

But I moved him for you. He's where no one will ever find him. I kept us safe, didn't I? But some nights, I wonder if it was the right thing. Maybe we should've called the police. Maybe there was another way. But then I think about Piper and how we couldn't let this destroy her. I did what had to be done to protect our family.

I know you're angry even if you won't say it. I see it in the way you look at me sometimes during your secret visits, like I'm a stranger. Like I've changed. But I haven't. I'm still the person who loves you the most, who would do anything for you. Even this.

Please don't be mad for too long. If you ever want to talk about it, I'm here. I know it's difficult carrying this with me, but I'd do it all again if it meant keeping you both safe.

This isn't over. Not for me, not for us. You understand, don't you? I'll be home soon and then I can keep protecting her. And you. Just like you deserve. Just like I always have.

You'll see.

Piper

The letter sat in my lap like a living thing. I knew the first one looked familiar and now the paper pulsed with a truth I wasn't ready to accept. The handwriting mocked me and taunted all the years I had trusted my father.

I hadn't seen it before but I knew it now. I recognised the way his letters curled and the way his words stretched across the page. My dad had written this, he must have done. He was the one who'd loved my mother. And he had done something terrible for her.

I read it at least five times, each word sinking deeper into my chest and making it tighten around my lungs. This meant it couldn't be Peter leaving me letters as a joke or to scare me. He wouldn't have the same handwriting. I traced the ink with my fingertip. The swirling letters matched the ones that had been tormenting me all week. It was the same loops, the same angles, the same hand. I knew it so well. I had spent years reading it on shopping lists, and reminders left on the fridge. My biggest chore as a teenager had been shopping for my parents, and I always went off with one of my dad's handwritten lists crumpled in my fist. It was his.

But my father was dead, and despite his faults he hadn't been a murderer. He was a quiet, forgiving man who always had a laugh and a treat for me. This couldn't be real. There was just no way he'd kill someone. But who else could it be? My mum was never seen with anyone else. She didn't love anyone else. And if it wasn't my dad's secret then whose was it? A chill ran down my spine as the final question clawed its way into my thoughts. Who the hell had they murdered?

Was that who I saw in my dreams? The boy they had taken from me? I paced the living room, gripping the letter like it might burst into flames if I let go.

Even if my father was somehow still alive and wrote those threatening notes to me then why? He wouldn't. It didn't make sense. None of this made sense.

He was a kind and stable man. If I was honest, he was the most boring man I knew. He did nothing remotely interesting. He certainly wouldn't have had a breakdown, murdered someone or faked his own death. Would he?

No. The thought was almost laughable. But then again, how well had I really known my parents? Not as well as most kids knew theirs. After the fire, I was lost and confused, scared. Without my memory, a part of me had been stripped away, leaving behind nothing but empty space.

I didn't remember a thing. Being collected from the hospital by two strangers who *said* they were my parents had been terrifying. I was supposed to trust them and believe in their words alone, because there were no pictures left to prove I was their daughter. How did I know they were telling the truth?

They were nice enough, but I had never truly trusted them. Not with my pre-teen life or with anything that came after. There was no bond, or if there had been, it burned away with my memories. They meant nothing to me. And I hated myself for it.

Mum had known. I could see it in the way she looked at me sometimes, like she resented me for not loving her back.

But the unwelcome question niggled at the edge of my thoughts. If it can't be my father writing these notes, what if it's me?

What if these letters aren't even real?

After all, the other two disappeared when I tried to show the detective. I stopped pacing and gripped the frame of the bed to steady myself. My breath came in shallow bursts as the memory fought its way to the surface. I'd told myself for years that I'd moved on, that I wasn't that girl anymore, but it's never that easy.

I was sixteen when the visions started. That little boy with wide, white eyes and a face that flickered in and out of focus. He'd appear when I was alone, watching me from the shadows. His small figure was sometimes outlined by flames that didn't seem to bother him.

I stopped wanting to come home from school and couldn't sleep at night. My parents dismissed my behaviour at first. Dad ignored it. He was good at that. Mum brushed it off as stress from my school exams. But it got worse over the next couple of years. I couldn't eat. I couldn't sleep. Eventually the boy was always there, even in my dreams, He whispered things I couldn't understand. He convinced me Dad wasn't really Dad and someone had taken over. Dad was a pretender, and he needed to die. And then, one night I couldn't take it anymore and I snapped.

I'd woken up in the hospital with bandages on my wrists and my parents hovering over me. My mum's expression was angry, as if I'd been ungrateful, whilst my dad was terrified. The doctor sent me away the next day to a locked hospital I couldn't get out of now matter how much I screamed at the staff to help me. Everyone was convinced I'd lost my mind.

I suffered three months in a psychiatric ward surrounded by people telling me I was crazy and I believed they must be right. Even now, I could feel it. The stigma, the doubt, and the fear. I must have been crazy to think someone evil had taken Dad over, and to see the boy everywhere I looked.

But was it happening again? I could be writing these letters and not even know it.

I had to get out of the bedroom. I ran downstairs and sank onto the sofa, clutching the letter tightly. My memory was already full of holes. There was a black void stretching back to almost my entire childhood. I'd survived a fire I didn't really remember. That was all I knew. But what if there were other things I'd forgotten?

I grabbed my phone, snapped a photo of the letter so it couldn't disappear this time, and then dialled Adam.

"Hey," he answered on the second ring, his voice warm.

I hesitated. He didn't need this. He had his patients and his own life. I shouldn't drag him into my chaos. But the words tumbled out anyway.

"I found another letter," I said, my voice shaking.

"What letter?" His tone shifted, full of concern.

"In my parents' room," I rushed on. "It was addressed to my mum. I think it's from my dad. But the handwriting is the same as the notes left on my car. It's *his* handwriting."

He didn't respond right away. The silence made my stomach churn.

"Piper," he said finally. "Think about this. That makes no sense."

"I know it doesn't!" I snapped. "It's his handwriting,

though. It's his words. I'm not imagining it!"

"Okay, okay," he blurted. "But think about it for a second. Why would your dad do that? He loved you, and... he's dead. Even if he was alive, why would he scare you like that? He wouldn't leave you creepy notes and then steal them. Doesn't that seem far-fetched?"

"I don't know why!" My voice cracked. "I just know it's his handwriting. It's the same style, the same words, the same sign off."

"Look, I'm not saying you're wrong." Adam sighed. "I'm just saying maybe there's another explanation. Are you absolutely sure you didn't write them yourself? Not on purpose."

"What?" I cut him off, my heart dropping. It couldn't be happening that the one person I thought I could rely on is accusing me of being crazy. "You think I wrote them? Are you serious?"

"I'm not accusing you," he said slowly. His tone was patronising, which only made me angrier. "But you've been under a lot of stress. Sometimes people lose time. Things happen, and they don't remember doing them. It's not unheard of, Piper. You know what happened to you before."

"Don't you dare psychoanalyse me right now," I hissed. I was suddenly regretting telling him about my past. "I know what I saw and I know what I read. It's his handwriting, Adam!"

He sighed again, softer this time.

"I'm just asking you to consider the possibility that this isn't what it seems. You've been through so much."

"Stop," I said sharply. "Just stop."

"Piper," he began, but I hung up before he could finish.

I paced the living room again with the phone still clutched in my hand. My thoughts were spinning so fast I could barely keep up. *Adam* thought I was crazy.

Did he think I'd planted the letters to scare myself? That I was having some sort of breakdown?

I rang him hoping he'd reassure me, but our conversation had only worried me further. I'd made mistakes before and let my mind twist and turn until I didn't know what was real anymore.

But this *was* real. It had to be.

Or was he right? Was I having a breakdown?

I shook my head, refusing to let the fear take root. Then I looked at the photo on my phone. It was there. I wasn't crazy. I sent it to Adam to show him I wasn't imagining this.

I grabbed my car keys and the letter and shoved it into my bag before heading out the door. I wasn't letting it go anywhere this time. The evening air was sharp, but it did nothing to clear the fog in my head. I climbed into the driver's seat and gripped the wheel tightly as I drove aimlessly through the dark streets.

The police station loomed ahead before I even realised I was heading there. Its harsh lights spilled across the pavement, making it look unwelcoming. I parked across the street and stared at it.

What was I doing?

I couldn't just walk in and hand them the letter. Even if it was Detective Swanson I spoke to. What would I say anyway? That my father confessed to a murder in a letter I found while clearing through Mum's things? That the handwriting matched the notes someone had been leaving on my car? Oh, and that he's dead.

He'd laugh me out of the building. Or worse, he'd believe me. They'd dig into my father's life, and my whole family's life. *My* life. What if I was wrong?

Who the hell was the note even talking about? If my gentle father really had murdered someone to protect me and Mum, then who would it be? I needed to find out who had died around that time or went missing. I pulled the letter back out of my handbag and searched it quickly for a date. It was written at the top.

18th May 2007

One month before the fire happened. I felt sick and leaned forward to rest my aching head against the steering wheel. My thoughts were a tangled mess of fear. Was the fire the aftermath of this murder?

I stared at the station and willed myself to move. The weight of the letter in my bag felt unbearable, like it might drag me down into the earth if I let it. If the police thought I was crazy, they'd lock me away again.

Minutes passed. Maybe hours. Eventually, I started the car and drove away. I allowed the station to disappear in my rearview mirror.

I didn't know where I was going. I just knew I couldn't go inside.

Summer

Oakleigh House was like many other community care homes Summer had visited in her previous life as a mental health advocate. It was an average, red-brick, detached house, though they tended to be on the larger side of average with at least five bedrooms. The brickwork was clean, winter flowers lined the small front garden, and the curtains in each window were uniform and tidy.

The home felt less personal inside. All the internal walls were painted a bland magnolia, the kind chosen more for ease of maintenance rather than warmth. The furniture in the dining room where she and Swanson had set up for the day was functional but plain. The room was bright due to the large bay window, but the thick atmosphere remained thanks to Hayley's disappearance.

Dr Andrew Metcalfe, the house psychiatrist, had finally called her back and agreed to let them speak to the residents, but only on the condition that she remained present for the duration of each interview. Summer sat next to each patient and reassured them she was there to support them, and Swanson sat opposite. His usual quiet intensity had been making the patients visibly fidgety all day.

They had got no new information out of anyone so far. The

last patient was a wiry man in his late forties with darting, restless eyes and a permanent furrow etched into his brow. His name, according to the file in Summer's lap, was Trevor Haines. His skin had the weathered look of someone who spent too much time outdoors despite his pale complexion, and his clothes, though clean, were mismatched. He clutched a battered novel in his hands. Every few moments, he glanced around the room, his lips moving soundlessly.

"Trevor," Swanson tried again. "Is there anything else you can tell us about Hayley?"

"Her hair always smells nice," Trevor said sadly as he looked back at Swanson.

"Okay. We'll keep that in mind." Swanson rose to his feet. "If there's nothing else, Trevor. It was nice meeting you."

"Wait!" Trevor said as he stood. "You didn't ask me about Perry."

"Perry?" replied Swanson, casting a glance at Summer.

"Yes. Perry Vance. He used to live here, but now he's a community client."

"What did you expect us to ask about him?" Swanson asked.

"Well, he's gone. I thought you'd ask if I know anything about his disappearance too."

Swanson tensed. His gaze flickered to Summer before returning to Trevor.

"And do you know anything about Perry Vance?" he asked slowly.

"He rang me to say he had to leave. He's scared of someone but I don't know who. He isn't scared of anyone in here. It's someone out there. That's why I want to stay right here. It's much safer. Do you want me to see if they have a spare bed for you, Dr Thomas?"

"No thank you, Trevor," Summer replied, hiding her smile.

"Did he say anything about this person he was scared of?" Swanson asked.

Trevor shook his head.

"Okay. Thanks anyway, Trevor."

"Come on. I'll walk you back to the kitchen. It smells good."

Summer led Trevor out of the room and returned a few minutes later. Swanson was already on his feet and holding out her coat. He had that same wired look in his eyes that he always got when something fired him up.

"Come on. Let's find out what's happening with Perry Vance."

* * *

Hours later, Summer leaned over her desk, rubbing the small of her back. The visit had been a dead end. Perry Vance wasn't home when she and Swanson arrived. And now her focus blurred between the page of notes in front of her and the steady voices drifting in from the station corridor. The baby had been unusually active all day, and the tiny feet jabbed at her ribs as if to remind her she needed a break.

"You alright, Summer?" Hart's voice carried through the office, sharp as usual. She strolled in with her short hair tousled as if she'd just got back inside.

"Just wishing this one would settle down for a bit." Summer smiled faintly. She placed a hand on her swollen belly, feeling another firm kick in response.

"Ah, a lively one, then. Takes after Swanson, probably having a tantrum." Hart smirked, dropping into the chair opposite her. "Speaking of your other half, he's on the phone with some stubborn administrator trying to get us into that mental health home Piper works in. Pinevale House. Thought I'd keep you in the loop while he bangs his head against a wall. It's quite funny to watch if you fancy a break."

"The other mental health home?" Summer raised her eyebrows at the thought of another full day of interviews.

"He's keen to follow it up." Hart leaned back in a chair and folded her arms. "See if we can make sense of it for Piper if she's not lying, but also see if it's linked to Hayley Smith and Perry Vance." "Do we know when Perry was last seen yet?" Summer straightened up.

"Last night," Hart said grimly. "He still has mental health carers who visit him and make sure he's okay in the community, like you suspected. Hayley Smith was one of his carers. He gets two visits a day, but wasn't in for either of them yesterday. He never misses them, apparently. It's part of his terms of being released. So the care home reported him missing officially today. They should have done it yesterday. I get the feeling Dr Metcalfe didn't want to report it."

"I'm guessing he didn't want us unsettling his patients further or giving the posh neighbours reason to complain."

"Well, Perry's phone is off, and we're treating it as urgent considering his mental health."

"And the other disappearance," Summer added.

Hart nodded, her mouth set in a grim line.

"Swanson thinks there might be a connection. Or Perry knows where Hayley is. We have nothing solid yet, but Perry disappearing doesn't sit right."

"Do you think someone has hurt him?" Summer asked, her voice quiet.

"It's a possibility. Or he's our man and he's on the run." Hart exhaled sharply, avoiding her gaze. "We'll know more when we dig into everything."

A tense silence fell between them before Hart pushed herself to her feet, clapping her hands.

"Anyway, I was about to do some more boring door-knocking around Pinevale House to see if the neighbours saw anyone leaving notes on cars. Swanson will appreciate it, and thought I'd see if you fancied coming along for a bit of fresh air. Unless you're chained to that desk."

Summer hesitated, glancing at the pile of reports in front of her. None of it felt as urgent as what Hart was doing. Besides, a change of scenery, and perhaps a chance to stretch her legs, might do her aching body some good.

"Sure," she said, rising slowly and grabbing her coat. "Joshua is with his Dad. They're doing football training tonight until eight."

"Nice. I could use the company. Swanson's no fun to drag around when he's in one of his moods."

"He takes brooding to a whole new level." Summer laughed.

The two women stepped out of the main office and into the hallway that led to the rear car park. Swanson stood near the far wall, phone pressed to his ear and his jaw tight. He caught Summer's eye and gave her a brief nod, his expression softening for a moment before he turned back to his call.

She smiled back at him, but as they stepped into the chilly evening air, she couldn't shake the growing unease settling in her stomach.

As they neared Hart's car, Summer's phone buzzed in her pocket. She fished it out, frowning at the private number on the screen. A flash of instinct told her to ignore it, but her thumb hit the green button before she'd made the decision.

"Hello?"

"Summer Thomas?"

"Yes, who's this?" she asked cautiously. The voice was familiar, though she couldn't place it.

"I think you need to know," the caller said slowly. "Your detective friend is looking in the wrong place."

"What do you mean? Who is this?" Summer froze, her pulse quickening.

"Try looking closer to home. Piper's home."

And then the owner of the voice hit her.

"Perry? Where are you? Are you okay?"

But the line went dead.

Piper

My knuckles ached from gripping the steering wheel too tight but I couldn't let go. I should've gone into the station. I should've handed over the old letters and let someone else deal with this.

But what if I was wrong and my greatest fear was coming true? I couldn't stop thinking about that day when the walls of reality had blurred and cracked until nothing made sense anymore. I had just told Mum and Dad about the little boy I'd been seeing that week.

Then I whispered into Mum's ear one night as she begged me to tell her what was wrong. I admitted I'd remembered something from before the fire. The boy was real. I told her he wasn't just a dream, but she didn't believe me.

Then I told her Dad wasn't Dad. The man living with us looked like Dad. He had the same eyes. The same nose. But it wasn't him. He wasn't the Dad from my memories.

I begged her not to say anything and to run away with me. Instead, she told Dad what I said, and they took me to the hospital. That's where white coats and funny shaped pills turned me into a ghost of myself. I hadn't seen the boy since then. So clearly he wasn't real, and the man in my memories must have never existed.

My heart thudded painfully as I pulled into the driveway of the same place the paramedics tore me from. Maybe Adam was about to do the same thing.

It took me a minute to notice his car was parked outside.

I cursed despite my heart lifting at the sight of his lean frame and floppy hair. I pulled up and stepped out into the cold with my bag firmly slung over my shoulder and made my way to the door.

"Hey," Adam said, his expression soft as he followed me up the drive.

"You got here fast," I said, stepping inside the house and allowing him inside.

"Yeah, I was already on my way when you called. I didn't have time to tell you."

"It's a two-hour drive. I only called you an hour ago."

"Traffic was light." He shrugged, his hands stuffed into his jacket pockets. "I might've pushed the speed limits a bit, but I wanted to see you."

"Right." My voice was tight.

I slipped past him into the kitchen. He followed me in, leaning against the counter as I dropped my bag onto a chair.

"What happened at the station?" he asked.

"I didn't go in," I admitted, avoiding his gaze.

"Why not?"

"I couldn't." My throat felt dry. "I kept thinking about what they'd say, what they'd think of me. Even you think this is in my head."

"Piper, I do not think you're crazy." He stepped closer, his hand brushing my arm.

I sniffed. I desperately wanted to believe him but the words felt like a lie. My dad had said the same thing before sending me away. He'd stood in the same kitchen, too. It was like déjà vu.

"I don't know anymore," I said, my voice trembling. "The letters really are the same handwriting, Adam. The ones on my car and now the ones addressed to my mum. That can't just be a coincidence. It's so weird."

"It could be." He frowned. "Or it really could be a lack of sleep and stress."

"Are you serious?" I snapped, stepping back. "You think my brain is making this up because I'm stressed? You don't think if I was making something up it would be something a bit more calming?"

"I didn't say that," he replied in a measured tone. "I just think we need to consider every possibility. You've been through a lot lately. Stress can do strange things to your mind."

"You sound just like them." My chest tightened, and I rubbed it with my palm.

"Sound like who?"

"My parents," I said, the words spilling out before I could stop them. "When I told Mum about the boy she acted like I was insane. She told Dad. They locked me up, Adam. They made me believe I was broken just because I remembered Dad differently and got scared."

His eyebrows shot up, and I realised I'd said the wrong thing. Adam knew about the suicide attempt, and he knew I'd seen a little boy as a vision sometimes that I still had dreams about. But he didn't know the full extent of how often I saw that little boy, nor my fears about a devil invading Dad.

"What do you mean you remembered him differently?"

"Nothing," I snapped as I shifted to my other foot.

"Baby, tell me."

His fingers grazed my cheek softly, and I looked up into his soft brown eyes. I sighed heavily and looked away. I didn't want to see the look on his face when he officially diagnosed me with whatever the hell was wrong with me.

"I can't explain how weird it was waking up as a ten-year-old with no memories of these two strangers who insisted they were my parents. It was terrifying."

"I can't even imagine."

"They were nice enough, but I felt so alone and so scared. Like I was constantly in fight-or-flight mode but I couldn't do either. I didn't know them, and I certainly didn't trust either of them. Why would I trust strangers? And I always felt like they were lying to me. There was something missing. Then when I was sixteen the little boy began appearing. By the time I was eighteen he was everywhere. Even as I slept, I dreamt of him. Eventually I realised the boy was a memory, not a hallucination. Or so I thought."

"And now?"

"Now I know he was a hallucination. I haven't seen him in years, other than in the fire dreams."

"And your dad?" Adam pushed.

"Well." I sighed again and rubbed my face. "I thought I had a memory of him too. Same eyes, same nose, same hair as the man who said he was my dad, but a different man."

Adam's face softened, but I didn't want his pity. I wanted him to believe me.

"Piper," he whispered. "You're not broken. You're just trying to make sense of everything, and that's okay. But maybe you're looking for connections that aren't really there."

My stomach clenched. Adam had been my last chance for someone to confirm I wasn't crazy. I took a step away from him. My gaze darted around the room. I couldn't go back there as a patient. I could run away before Adam called an ambulance. Or had he already called them without me knowing? That's what Mum did. Were they on the way?

That's when I saw it.

The corner of the room darkened behind Adam. The edges of the darkness shifted, shifting into a shape. My pulse raced as I stared at the moving shadow.

Adam was talking, but I couldn't hear what he was saying. Slowly, the shadow took shape. A figure no taller than a child stepped out of the gloom to join us.

The boy.

His blurred face turned toward me, and I fought the urge to scream. I couldn't see his features, but I could see his blank eyes were unblinking as he stared at me. He didn't move or speak. He just watched.

"Piper?" Adam's sharp tone broke through the haze.

I blinked and glanced at him. When I looked back at the corner, the boy was gone.

"What is it?" Adam asked, stepping forward.

"Nothing. It's nothing." I shook my head, my hands trembling.

"Piper, talk to me," he said, his voice firm now.

"I can't do this." The words burned my throat. "I need you to go."

"What?" His face twisted with confusion.

"I need you to go back to Harrogate," I said. My voice cracked, and I swallowed back tears. "I just need space."

"Piper, come on," he said. I'd never heard him sound so frustrated. "I came all this way to be with you so you aren't dealing with this alone."

"Please." My voice broke on the word.

"Fine." He stared at me for a moment, his jaw tightening, then he grabbed his keys from the counter. "If that's what you want, I'll go."

I didn't answer. I couldn't even look at him as he walked to the door.

"I love you, Piper," he whispered as he stood in the doorway.

"I know."

I swallowed hard, my chest aching. He thinks he loves me, but if he knew I was seeing the boy again, would he still? The front door clicked shut, and I was alone.

But I didn't feel alone.

I felt watched.

Piper

fter Adam left, the silence in the house was suffocating again. It pressed against me as I curled on the sofa with a glass of wine in hand. Or maybe it was the fourth glass. I wasn't counting. The bottle of white perched on the coffee table was pretty much empty. It was a poor substitute for the calm I was desperate to feel.

The boy wasn't real.

I knew that now because he hadn't aged. Not like me. I repeated the thought like a mantra, gripping the stem of the glass so hard my knuckles turned white. He couldn't be real. My mind was just playing tricks on me because of stress. That's all it was.

"Get a grip, Piper," I muttered, running a hand through my tangled hair.

I leaned back into the cushions and stared blankly at the dark TV screen. My reflection stared back. I was pale and hollow-eyed with shadows under my cheekbones. I looked as bad as I felt. The wine was supposed to help, but it wasn't doing the trick. Maybe what I needed was a reset. I could have a shower. It would be something to wash away the tension clinging to my skin.

Dragging myself up, I shuffled to the bathroom, leaving my

glass on the edge of the sink as I turned on the tap. Cold water spilled out. It splashed over my hands and pooled in the basin. I cupped some in my palms and pressed it to my face, gasping at the sharp chill.

When I looked up at the mirror, I hardly recognised myself. My skin was so pale it looked almost translucent, and my hair hung in limp, messy strands.

"You're fine," I told my reflection. "Just tired."

The shower blasted to life with a satisfying hiss. Steam curled around me as I stripped off my clothes and stepped inside. The hot water poured over me, both scalding and soothing at the same time. The world disappeared, and I held on to peace for a few blessed moments.

I felt better when I finally turned the water off and stepped out. Wrapping a towel around myself, I padded to the bedroom to change into a pair of comfortable leggings and an oversized jumper. I allowed the soft fabric and warmth to cocoon me into a sense of safety. The house was quiet when I returned to the kitchen.

But as I switched on the light, I froze. Something was wrong. The wine bottle was gone. Had I put it away? No. I would've remembered that. Wouldn't I?

I turned toward the kitchen. And my stomach dropped. The chairs were on the table. The floor glistened with fresh streaks of water, the smell of lemon cleaner faint in the air. Someone had cleaned. Someone had been in here.

I took a shaky step forward, my breath hitching when I noticed the kitchen counter. The missing letters were back.

Someone had scattered both of the letters that were left on my car, plus the newest one from my handbag, onto the countertop. They'd opened each envelope and laid out each letter in a haphazard mess.

"No," I whispered, my voice trembling.

This couldn't be happening. I hadn't done this.

Had I?

I could still smell a faint whiff of Adam's aftershave, and I suddenly longed for him to be with me. Regret hit me for making him leave. I reached for one of the bits of paper with trembling fingers. I needed to see if it was real.

I inhaled sharply when my fingers touched the paper. They were definitely real. The handwriting, Dad's handwriting, leapt out at me.

But I couldn't focus on the words. My mind spun. I stumbled back and gripped the edge of the table for support. The image of the boy standing behind Adam flashed through my mind. I could still see the way his wide, unblinking eyes bored into me.

"No," I said again, louder this time as if it would help make everything go back to normal somehow.

The house remained silent; the letters spread out taunting me. I turned slowly and scanned the room, half-expecting to see him again. But he was nowhere to be seen.

"You're not real," I whispered as I clutched my arms around myself.

The silence didn't answer. My gaze shifted back to the table as a sick feeling twisted in my stomach. The letters looked exactly as I remembered them. Two new and one yellowed with age, both sets of handwriting painfully familiar.

But then my eyes caught on something that didn't belong. There was another one. An extra letter sitting apart from the others. The envelope was unopened, its edges crisp. And again they'd addressed it directly to me.

The Shadow

*P*iper,

   Did you think I wouldn't notice? That I wouldn't see? You've been sloppy. You've been careless, even. Walking around as if you're untouchable, like the cracks in you aren't splitting wider every day. You left the door open. You let someone in. I don't think you understand the weight of that mistake.

   You brought him here. Into our space. Into what's mine.

   I've watched him. The way he moves, the way he looks at you. It's pathetic, really. You think he's strong, don't you? That he can protect you? But you're wrong. He's a shadow of something you think you need. A placeholder.

   You've always been like this. Grasping for things you can't hold on to, trusting the wrong people. It's a wonder you've survived this long considering how little you pay attention.

   Do you even realise what's circling you? What's just waiting for you to stumble?

   You've been playing house, settling in, pretending this is all normal. But you're not normal, Piper. You never have been.

   You think I don't remember? You know I remember everything. I know every inch of this house. I know what you've touched, what you've changed, what you've tried to erase. But you can't erase me.

I know where you've been, what you've been doing. I saw you at the station today, sitting in your car, watching the entrance like a scared little girl. Did you think going there would make you feel safe? That talking to them would solve anything?

You're wasting time. You can't stop what's coming.

I see you, Piper. Every second of every day, I'm there, just out of reach, waiting for the moment you slip. Because you will slip. You always do.

And when you do, I'll be there to pick up the pieces.

Stop looking for answers in the wrong places. You already know the truth. It's in you, buried so deep you're too scared to dig it up. But I'll help you. I'll help you remember.

You'll see.

P.S. I like the new paint colour for the living room. Well done. Proud of you.

Swanson

Swanson was driving home to Darley Abbey when his phone buzzed. The screen lit up with Piper Roberts' name. He frowned at it. He hadn't heard from her since he visited. She was probably after an update. He picked up quickly with the car's built-in hands free.

"Swanson," he answered.

"Alex Swanson? It's Piper Roberts." Her voice was shaky. "I need you. Please. Someone's been inside my house."

"Piper, slow down." He kept his voice even. "What's happened?"

"I'm freaking out," she continued, her words coming in a breathless rush. "I came downstairs and things were out of place. Someone mopped my floor and binned my wine bottle."

"Okay," Swanson replied slowly. Mopped the floor? Binned a bottle? Maybe Hart was right about poor Piper. Maybe she needed Summer's help more than she needed his.

"And the chairs were all moved around. The worst part is the missing letters. They're back. Someone left them the table. All of them, plus a new one."

Swanson's brow furrowed as he sat up straighter.

"Just breathe. I'll come over and check it out. Stay where you are, okay? I am right near your house, anyway."

"Please hurry," she whispered. Her voice broke. "I don't know what to think."

"Don't worry," Swanson replied quickly. "I'm on my way."

He drove fast. His house was only a few streets away from Piper. Not that he would tell her that. But Piper's tone worried him. It wasn't just paranoia. She sounded genuinely terrified. She needed some sort of help, whether it was the police she needed, or medical help.

When he pulled up outside her house a few minutes later, the street was eerily quiet. He parked up, climbed out of the car and took in a quick scan of the area. There was nothing out of the ordinary that he could see. Satisfied, he approached the front door and rapped firmly.

"Piper? It's me, Alex Swanson."

The door opened almost immediately. Piper looked like she hadn't slept in days. Her eyes were bloodshot against pale skin. Her wet hair was a tangled mess. The oversized hoodie she wore was rumpled as if she'd been clutching it for dear life.

"Come in," she said, stepping back to let him inside. She hugged her arms around herself as if trying to hold everything together.

Swanson stepped into the hallway, his gaze sweeping the space. The air smelled faintly of lemon. "Show me what this is about then," he said. He kept his tone gentle but direct. He might have to convince poor Piper to come to a hospital, after all.

She led him down the short hallway and into the kitchen. The room felt normal. The chairs were perched neatly on the table as if someone had cleaned around them, and the floor glistened faintly with a damp sheen. That's where the faint smell of cleaner was coming from. Piper hovered by the counter, where he saw letters scattered across the wooden surface.

"They weren't here before I went upstairs for a shower," she murmured. "I swear, they were gone."

Swanson approached the counter to study the letters. There were three. Two of the envelopes had Piper's name scrawled across the front in sharp, angular handwriting. So they did exist. Another was blank.

"Have you touched anything?" he asked.

"Just the new letter," she said, her voice shaking as she pointed to one of the named envelopes. "I couldn't help it."

"And you're certain none of this was like this when you went to shower?" Swanson glanced over at her.

"Yes!" she snapped. "I was in the living room all night before that. The chairs were normal, the floor was sticky because I spilled some wine, and those letters weren't here."

"Okay," he said slowly, his voice steady. "Let's focus on the new letter. Did you read it?"

She nodded, biting her lip.

"It's worse this time. Whoever wrote it, they know things about the house and who's been in here."

"May I?" Swanson gestured toward the letter as he pulled on some gloves.

Piper hesitated for a moment before picking it up and handing it to him. Her hands trembled as she released the paper. He took it out of the envelope and unfolded it carefully, his eyes scanning the words. The handwriting was clean and precise, but the tone was strange. It was protective, but threatening.

Did you think I wouldn't notice? That I wouldn't see? You've been sloppy. You brought him here. Into our space. Into what's mine.

"Who did you bring round?" he asked.

"My boyfriend, Adam Bell, was here. He's gone now."

"Hmm." He reached out for the letter, and his gaze flicked to Piper. "The new paint in the living room?"

"I bought it last week. It's next to the sofa. No one else knew except Adam. At least so I thought. Whoever wrote this must have seen it when they broke in."

"Any sign of a break in?"

"Nothing. I have no idea how they got into the house."

"We need to talk to Adam," Swanson said firmly as he folded the letter and placed it back on the counter. "Does he have a key to the house?"

"No. No one does," she replied. "I don't have a spare. It got lost ages ago."

"You should change the locks."

"Wait, the lawn," she blurted. "Someone mowed it before I moved in."

"They mowed it?"

"Yes." She paused, her brow furrowing. "The front and back, and you can't reach the back without going through the house. I forgot all about it to be honest with everything going on."

"Who did you think it was at the time?"

"I thought it was the old neighbour. Norris Bale. He's creepy, and I caught him looking over the back fence on the day I moved in. He had a ladder leant against it and seemed annoyed. Then he was rude to Adam as well."

"Okay." Swanson's jaw tightened as he remembered the call Summer received from Perry Vance telling them to look closer to home. "We need to document this and talk to Norris Bale as well as Adam. I'll call it in, and we might get someone here to dust for prints as it might be connected to a bigger case."

"What case?"

Swanson hesitated. He really shouldn't have said that, but it needed to be said at some point. He rubbed his beard before answering.

"A missing mental health support worker."

"Hayley Smith? I saw on the news. What does she have to do with me?"

"Nothing, probably. I just need to explore all angles and you have the same job role. That's all. It could be a patient that's connected to both homes, for example. I'll need to take the letters with me."

"There's Michael to consider too," she blurted the name as if she's been considering keeping it to herself.

"Michael?"

"Yes. Michael Grey. He killed my parents. I think he's locked away though."

"Yes. I know about Michael Grey. I'll check it out and make sure he's still locked away."

"Do you think they'll find something?" Piper's eyes widened.

"Maybe," he said. "But right now, you can't stay here. Whoever's doing this knows too much about you, and we don't know if it's connected to Hayley's disappearance or not."

Her face crumpled, and Swanson thought she might argue. But then she nodded.

"I'll pack a bag."

"Good. I'll wait here while you do," he said as he stepped into the hallway to give her some space.

His mind raced as he stood there. The letters had unsettled him more than he wanted to admit. Whoever was watching Piper wasn't just trying to scare her. They were making it clear that this was personal. They could be watching them as he stood there.

Either that, or Hart was right about her not being well and Piper had written them herself.

When she returned, she had a small duffel bag slung over her shoulder, and her pale face was determined. He felt a twinge of guilt for thinking she might be the writer when she was so obviously terrified. He gave her a reassuring nod.

"We'll figure this out," he said. "I promise."

As they stepped outside, the chilly night air pressed in around them. Piper made her way to her car as he watched. He scanned the street, and his eyes narrowed at the empty window of the neighbouring house where Norris Bale lived. The feeling of being watched prickled the back of his neck. He couldn't see anything, but someone was out there. He could feel their stare. And if he didn't find out who soon, he had the sinking feeling Piper wouldn't be the only one in danger.

The Boys

The night air carried a sharp chill as two boys walked along a dimly lit street. The smaller boy trailed slightly behind with his head down. His hands were stuffed into the pockets of his too-thin jacket. The instigator walked ahead with a more confident stride. His eyes constantly scanned the darkened houses that lined the street.

They stopped in front of a modest two-story home halfway down the road. The smaller boy hesitated and glanced nervously at his companion.

"Are you sure about this?" he whispered, his voice trembling.

The instigator turned to him, his face hard.

"We made a deal. You said you wanted them gone after what they did to you. This is how you make it happen. Unless you've changed your mind?"

"No. I haven't." The smaller boy swallowed hard as he shook his head.

"Good." The other boy's lips curved into a stiff smile. "Then stay out here and I'll take care of it. You don't even have to do anything."

The smaller boy's breath caught in his throat as he watched his companion slip around the side of the house. He moved so quickly. He stood frozen in the shadows, his heart pounding in his chest and every instinct screaming at him to run. But he couldn't move.

This was what he'd wanted, wasn't it? To finally be free of the people who made his life unbearable?

Minutes passed like hours, and the silence stretched tautly until a muffled thud broke it from inside the house. He flinched, his stomach twisting with fear.

The instigator reappeared at the side of the house. He looked different then. He wasn't as calm. His face was flushed and his breathing was heavy. He motioned for the other boy to follow him.

"Come on," he said, his voice urgent. "It's done."

The smaller boy hesitated. His feet were rooted to the ground.

"What did you do to them?" he asked.

"You'll see." The instigator's smile widened. "Come on. I'll show you before we go."

His feet wouldn't move at first. The house wasn't just quiet. It felt wrong. As if the walls knew what had just happened or the air was holding its breath.

Then, reluctantly, the smaller boy followed him inside. They walked through a dark kitchen to the living room. It was eerily quiet, and the air was heavy with a metallic smell. Then he saw his parents.

They lay slumped on the couch. Their bodies were completely still. He couldn't see his dad's face. He was bent over, face almost on his knees. But his mother lay on her back on the sofa. Her wide, glassy eyes stared back at him. Blood trailed down her face from the biggest gash he'd ever seen in her head.

The smaller boy stared at them. His body froze. His mind struggled to process what he was seeing. His mother's eyes blurred in and out of focus. He blinked rapidly, but she didn't change. She was still looking at him, and she would never stop. His stomach lurched. The smell of metal coated his tongue. He swayed. He wanted to run, scream, wake up.

"They can't hurt you anymore," the bigger boy said. His tone was more gentle than it had been. "You're free from them."

The smaller boy's chest tightened as a surge of conflicting emotions crashed over him. Relief. Horror. Guilt. Gratitude.

"Why did you do it?" he whispered as if his parents might hear him.

The boy shrugged. "Because we're the same, you and me. And I know when it's my turn, you'll do the same for me."

The smaller boy nodded slowly. The weight of the pact settled heavily on his shoulders. There was no getting away from it now. They were bonded for life. The smaller boy felt it clamp around his throat like a collar, or a chain. This was a deal he hadn't realised he'd signed. There was no backing out now. They belonged to each other.

Piper

I barely remember how I fell asleep after I reached the Pocket Stay Hotel. Exhaustion had finally hit me after the week from hell and smothered the panic just enough for my body to shut down. I'd locked the door, pushed a chair under the handle, and lay on the bed staring at the cracked ceiling. The shadows moved across it like creeping fingers, and I prayed they wouldn't take the shape of a little boy.

I brought the letter addressed to Mum with me and placed it on the desk. I'd hidden it before Swanson arrived. If he read it he'd assume Dad was a murderer, and I needed to figure that part out for myself first. I had to come to terms with what that would mean. I hadn't even read the others addressed to my mother yet.

Swanson left with a promise to call me Friday morning, but everything felt like it was slipping out of reach. The letters. The house. The boy. The white walls of the psychiatric hospital and the numb haze of medication were looking almost inviting.

Somehow, I must have passed out, because the next thing I knew, I was waking up groggily. It was five thirty a.m., and the world outside was still dark. I'd cracked the window open before settling down, and when I woke it let in a chill that bit at my skin.

So I sat up to close it. The bed groaned beneath me as I moved, and dizziness hit me. My head felt fuzzy, like I was swimming through the fog. I was probably dehydrated. Or needed to eat. I froze until it cleared enough to stand, then slowly dragged myself to the window. I reached through the curtains to grab the handle, and they fell back just enough for me to peer out.

And my breath caught in my throat.

There, in the dim light of the car park, was the boy.

He stood motionless, half-hidden between two cars. His skinny frame cast an unnaturally long shadow across the ground. His face was indistinct, but his wide eyes seemed to cut straight through me.

I froze, the world around me pressing in like a vise. There was no way this was real. No way.

My hands shook as I gripped the windowsill. My mind really was breaking down again.

No.

"Fuck this," I muttered under my breath.

I pushed the panic down and forced myself into motion. I didn't care about the consequences anymore. Whatever this was, whatever it had become, I would not sit in a hotel room pretending it wasn't happening. I was not a terrified eighteen-year-old any more.

I pulled my coat on, grabbed my bag, and didn't look back. I didn't even think about what I was doing. I had to know what was going on, why the letters were showing up, why this boy kept appearing.

So I made my way back to the house.

The drive back was a bit of a blur. My thoughts spun out of control, each one worse than the last, but I didn't stop. The house was still as I pulled up. There was an eerie quiet surrounding it like a thick mist. The street was silent. All the neighbours' windows were dark.

I shoved the car into park and got out quickly, my heart pounding in my chest. I half-expected the boy to be standing somewhere waiting for me, but the driveway was empty.

I grabbed my keys and stormed into the house. The door felt heavier than usual. The darkness inside swallowed me whole as I stepped in. I quickly turned on the light and felt relief flood me.

I stormed upstairs. My steps echoed louder than usual through the quiet house. The remaining letters were still on my parents' bed where I'd left them. The sight of them sent a tremor of fear through me, but I forced myself forward. I couldn't avoid this anymore.

With trembling hands, I grabbed the envelopes and sat on the edge of the bed. The first envelope felt heavier than it should, the paper rough under my fingers. I hesitated. The truth was here in my hands. Whatever it was, I had to face it.

I pulled out the first letter and unfolded it. The words blurred as the past closed in and pulled me deeper. My gaze caught on a single phrase that burned into my mind.

You'll see.

The Shadow

My love,
　　I know you've always tried to shield yourself from the truth, but it's time you face it. That your daughter is not what you thought or hoped for. You think the fire was an accident, a tragic outburst or something out of her control, don't you? But it wasn't.

It wasn't her fault exactly. Not really. But it wasn't an accident either.

It happened because she is lost without me. You've been too focused on keeping everything perfect, trying to protect her from the world and from me by making me go away and moving house. You've never understood how much she needs more than just your love. She needs someone who can see the truth. She needs me.

Yes, the fire was terrible. But it wasn't evil. She isn't like him. It was just a sign. A sign that she can't live without me. We're a pair even if you don't like it when we kiss. You've always hated when we got too close, when she chooses me over you. Even now, you can't stand how much she still feels my touch. You never liked the way she looked at me. The way she reached for my hand first. The way she clung to my words instead of yours.

She'll never truly forget me. You can't see it, but you know it deep down. So does she, even now she can't remember.

You can't save her on your own. You're trying, but you're not enough. It's time you let someone else take the reins. Let me protect her, let me help her grow. I will make sure she learns the right lessons, and one day, she will look back at the fire and see it for what it was. A show of her love for me.

Please, trust me. I will keep her safe. I will guide her. I will protect her. You don't have to do this alone.

Piper is not beyond saving, not yet. But the time is coming. She's already beginning to remember. Soon, she'll come back to me. She'll understand. Soon, you will too.

You'll see.

Summer

It didn't surprise Summer to see that Swanson was already downstairs by the time she woke up. He wasn't sleeping properly lately; too worried about finding Hayley Smith and protecting Piper Roberts. And Summer knew he hated she was also getting those weird phone calls from missing Perry Vance.

Since Aunt Barb's murder, and everything else that happened last year, Swanson didn't really want Summer involved in anything dangerous. He'd be the same way with Hart, if she wouldn't punch him in the face for trying to be overprotective.

Then there was the fact that impending fatherhood must be playing on his mind. Summer wasn't worried about whether he'd be a good dad. She knew he'd be fantastic. He was amazing with Joshua. But Swanson was hard on himself. Too much so. And his own dad didn't set the best example.

She got out of bed and showered before getting dressed in smart black trousers and a pale yellow blouse. By the time she got downstairs, Joshua had finished eating his cereal and was laughing with Swanson.

"Go get dressed, Joshua," she said after acknowledging them both, eager for the little boy to be out of earshot while she checked on Swanson.

Joshua pulled a fed up face but ran off upstairs to get into his school uniform.

"I'm fine," Swanson answered her question without her having to ask it.

He stood up and put his arms around her. She leant against his chest, enjoying his warmth for a moment before pulling away.

"So, any leads?" she asked.

"One or two. Hart is going to check out a nosy neighbour Piper mentioned. Norris Bale. That might be what the call you received was about to look closer to home. Perry obviously knows something. I just can't see how it's connected. There's the boyfriend, Adam Bell, to talk to. Then I need to find out where Michael Grey is as he was transferred from prison to a mental health hospital somewhere not long after he was arrested."

"Let me do that part," she offered.

"That would be great."

"Mum! I can't find any clean pants!" Joshua yelled from the top of the stairs.

She sighed heavily. "I'll get on it right after I've dropped this one at school. Hopefully, with some pants on."

* * *

One hour later, Summer arrived at the police station. Her phone buzzed, and a text from Hart flashed up.

'Grey was moved to Nottingham Psychiatric Hospital. I tried to call, but the lady said he was no longer there. Swanson said you wanted to look into it?'

Swanson was already in the station somewhere, probably

with Hart in his office, but rather than finding them she went straight to the office space to find a spare desk to work from. It was easier sometimes to be alone than trying to work with those two bickering.

It was unusually quiet again. A lot of the officers were in the briefing room with DCI Jane Murray leading. Hopefully, she'd dragged them in there because there was a new lead on the case. Maybe Swanson and Hart were inside.

She set down her bags and hung her jacket on the back of the chair, along with her woolly hat. Grabbing her phone, she googled the number for Nottingham Psychiatric Hospital and hit dial.

"Good morning, Nottingham Hospital," a woman said.

"Hi, there. My name is Dr Summer Thomas. I work for Derbyshire Police. I need to get hold of one of your ex-patients. His name is Michael Grey."

"Oh, I'm not sure I can give that information out over the phone," the woman replied. "But if you can visit us with some ID, then I'm sure we could help you locate him."

"Sure, I'll be there within the hour," Summer replied.

At least it would get her out of the station. She sent Swanson a quick text.

I need to visit the psychiatric hospital to show my ID. They won't release his whereabouts otherwise.

The reply came seconds later.

Not without me.

She shook her head. You'd think she was made of glass rather than pregnant. She wasn't even going to talk to anyone other than the staff.

I'll be in the car park in two minutes. I will leave without you if you're not there.

By the time she'd put on her coat and hat and walked through the station, Swanson was waiting in the car park. She grinned at him.

"Hey look, it's my very own police bodyguard."

"You're looking into the whereabouts of a crazed gunman. There's no way you're doing that alone."

Summer rolled her eyes and got into the car. She set off, gripping the wheel with one hand and cranking up the heat with the other, glancing at Swanson out of the corner of her eye. He sat in the passenger seat, arms crossed, staring out of the window with his usual thoughtful scowl.

"You know," she started. "You could make this whole 'bodyguard' thing a little less broody. Maybe crack a smile now and then. I know you can do it. I've seen those lips twitch before."

Swanson grunted, his lips twitching briefly before settling back into their neutral line.

"I'll smile when we catch a break on this case."

"That's fair enough."

The morning sun was just beginning to burn through the low-hanging clouds, casting the smallest bit of warmth into the air. It wasn't enough for Summer. She cranked up the heating even further, much to Swanson's distaste.

"So, this whole Michael Grey lead, what if he's not involved?" Summer asked. "What if we're barking up the wrong tree?"

"Then we cross it off and move on to the next one," Swanson replied. "But something's not sitting right. The timing of his transfer, wherever he is, then the letters, too. It's too much to ignore. Piper said her boss died a few weeks ago so I looked into it. Her name was Evelyn Beeley. Someone shot her too. It happened in Harrogate. She was in her car. Piper was in the passenger seat and saw the whole thing happen."

"Jeez, and after what happened to her parents too? That poor woman."

"No one's been caught for it yet. They actually suspected Piper for a bit seeing as she was the only one in the car. She told them she hadn't seen the shooter. She'd been looking the other way at a young boy, but CCTV didn't show any kids around."

"Did it catch the shooter?"

"No. The CCTV was outside a shop and only showed one side of the street. The same side Piper was looking at from the passenger window, not the side of the driver where the shooter appeared from."

"Ugh. Typical. I hate feeling like we're always one step behind." Summer sighed, her hands tightening on the wheel.

"That's what this job is like," Swanson said, his voice softening.

They lapsed into silence, each lost in their own thoughts. Swanson leaned back in his seat, his fingers tapping lightly on the armrest. Then Summer slammed on the brake.

The tyres screeched as the car jolted to a halt and threw both of them forward against their seat belts.

"What the hell, Summer?" Swanson barked, his hand bracing against the dashboard as his eyes flicked to her stomach. "What's wrong?"

Her wide eyes locked onto the figure ahead. A man sauntered along the pavement, his clothes rumpled, and his hair wild.

"That's him," she yelled, pointing. "Look! That's Perry Vance."

Swanson followed her gaze, his sharp eyes narrowing as he studied the man.

"Stay here," he ordered, already unclipping his seat belt and reaching for the door handle.

"Swanson, wait!" Summer yelled, but he was already out of the car.

He left his door open in his hurry to get out, and she watched as he approached the man with deliberate, measured steps. He made sure his hands were visible, and his tone was calm.

"Perry Vance?"

Perry froze mid-step, his head snapping up like a startled animal. His eyes darted around, searching for an escape.

"It's Alex Swanson from Derbyshire Police. We met earlier this week. Can I have a word?"

"I don't know you," he muttered, his voice hoarse. "I didn't do anything."

"We know you didn't," Swanson said, keeping his tone steady. "We just want to talk. That's all. You're not in trouble."

Perry took a step back, his body coiled as if ready to bolt.

"Leave me alone," he said sharply, his voice trembling. "I can't go back. He'll find me."

"No one's going to hurt you, Perry. I promise." Swanson raised his hands in a gesture of reassurance. "But we need to know what you know. We need to keep you safe."

"Safe? You think I'm safe? You have no idea." Perry shook his head. Summer could tell he was about to bolt. She opened the driver's door and stepped out.

"Perry," she called gently, walking around the car to stand a few feet behind Swanson. "It's okay. We're here to help you. Do you remember me?"

Perry's eyes flicked to her, his expression shifting from panic to uncertainty.

"Yes. I know you."

"Then you know my name Dr Thomas. I work with DI

Swanson," she said softly. "We've been looking for you because we're worried about you. We just want to help."

"I don't need help," Perry snapped, but his voice wavered. "You don't understand. He's everywhere."

"Then let us understand," Summer said. She took a small step closer. "Come with us. We can talk at the station, and we'll make sure no one can hurt you there."

Perry hesitated, his eyes darting between them. Swanson stayed silent for once and allowed Summer to take the lead.

"We can't protect you out here," she continued. "But if you come with us we can figure this out together. You're not alone, Perry."

For a moment, it seemed like he might refuse. Then his shoulders slumped, and the tension drained out of his body.

"Okay," he whispered. "But if he finds me—"

"He won't," Swanson said firmly. "We'll make sure of it."

Perry nodded reluctantly, and Swanson gestured toward the car. Summer opened the back door and stepped aside to let him climb in. He moved slowly with his head down. When he sat, his hands fidgeted nervously in his lap. As Swanson slid into the passenger seat next to him, he glanced at Summer.

"Nice work," he whispered.

"Couldn't let you have all the fun," she replied, her voice light despite the knot of anxiety in her chest. She started the car, pulling back onto the road to head to Derby. Michael Grey would have to wait.

Piper

I sat at the kitchen table as I gripped one of Mum's letters and one of mine. I compared them carefully, despite feeling like I was losing my grip on reality. This letter had clearly been sent after the fire. It's the last one the writer sent. Or at least the last one Mum kept. The ones before talk about love. This one accuses my mother of getting rid of him.

She wanted to get me away from this murderer. But if my dad was the one who wrote these, he didn't go anywhere. Not that I remember. And surely there's no way I was setting fires and kissing people at less than ten years old. I only ever remembered being a good kid and doing as I was told. But I supposed my memory was the one thing I couldn't rely on.

I swallowed hard. My chest tightened as the doubt seeped in. My thoughts spiralled and tumbled over one another with increasing speed. I went through everything I knew to be true.

My parents were murdered. They were shot at close range as they walked down Cathedral Street holding hands. Their killer was a man called Michael Grey. He'd been suffering from serious psychosis, and they were not the only people he shot at. He injured two others.

The shooting was random. They didn't deserve it. There was no real reason or explanation. There was just violence and destruction, and his actions left me completely alone in the world. Until I met Adam two years later, almost one year ago to the day.

What he did was murder, but he wasn't found guilty of that. Officially, Michael Grey admitted to manslaughter on diminished responsibility. They'd locked him away in prison at first, but they sent him to Nottingham Psychiatric Hospital after his trial for treatment and handed him to the doctors there. It was the one place I had to avoid working after joining the local bank agency of mental health care workers, which was a job which sent me to any hospitals or community homes who were short-staffed. I couldn't bear the thought of coming face-to-face with him, someone who had torn apart my life in such a brutal and senseless way.

Though maybe their murder wasn't as senseless as we all thought. Maybe Michael Grey knew my parents after all, and the other people he shot were just a decoy.

Could the author of these letters be Michael Grey? I'd shut that thought down immediately before. But now, with everything that was happening, I wasn't so sure.

Fuck it.

I dialled the number for Nottingham Psychiatric Hospital. The call rang a few times before someone picked up.

"How can I help you?" The lady's voice was calm, which felt strange when my mind was in such a frenzy.

"I'm calling about a patient," I said, my voice tight. "Michael Grey. I'm his new mental health advocate, and I just wanted to check if he is up for a visit today as planned at ten a.m. "

There was a slight pause followed by the sound of typing. Then the woman returned to the call.

"I'm sorry, ma'am. There is no appointment. Michael Grey

is no longer a patient here."

My heart stopped. The room tilted beneath me. My vision blurred as I struggled to stay upright. "What do you mean? He was locked away! He's supposed to be in your care."

"I'm sorry," the woman repeated. "We released Michael Grey some time ago. He transferred to a community home. I'm afraid I can't provide further information about his current location over the phone."

Transferred to the community? My blood ran cold. I couldn't process the sudden new reality. Michael Grey was no longer under lock and key. He was out there somewhere, walking around free. And I didn't know where. My throat went dry.

"You can't tell me where he is? As his advocate I need to make sure he's okay."

"I'm afraid not, ma'am. For privacy reasons, I can't disclose that information."

I felt like I was going to collapse. It all was too much. I hung up the phone without another word. He was supposed to be locked up. He was supposed to be behind hospital bars. But now he was out there walking around after only three years by pretending to be sane.

I couldn't even begin to wrap my mind around that.

I tugged at my hair, wrapping it around my finger as I paced in tight circles. I needed to find him. If he was the one who knew my mother, who was angry at her and now obsessed with me, I couldn't just sit here and wait for him to make his next move. I needed to understand what really went on between him and my parents.

I couldn't be the victim again. Not when I felt so close to finding the answers. I grabbed my jacket. There was no point wasting any more time thinking about it or staring at words on a page. I went to the car and gripped my phone tightly in my hand, my fingers numb as I dialled Swanson's number. Maybe the hospital would tell him where Grey had gone. The phone rang and rang and eventually went to voicemail again.

Damn it, Swanson. Please pick up.

My finger hovered over Adam's name in my contacts list, but I threw the phone to the passenger seat. Adam wouldn't want to hear from me after what I said to him.

He was safer away from me.

I was on my own in this. Alone in a mess I didn't know how to fix. I couldn't trust anyone, not when it felt like the world around me was slowly crumbling apart.

The authorities had to know where Grey was after what he did. I spent the next couple of minutes searching online looking for a photo or a news article. Something. Anything. But after quickly scrolling past the image of my parents that haunted me from the news for months after their deaths, all I found was the same outdated information about his arrest, trial, and commitment to Nottingham Psychiatric Hospital. There was nothing new.

Maybe I should've been glad that he was out of the hospital. His release meant he'd supposedly been treated, and he was no longer a danger to himself or others. It meant that he was "fit for reintegration". But all I could think about was how terrifyingly easy it would be for him to slip under the radar.

Or to find me.

There had to be someone who could help me. Someone who could give me an answer. I wasn't even sure the police would take the lead seriously. I had no proof that Michael Grey was connected to any of this. Swanson wouldn't have anything to go on.

Then I saw a woman behind me leaving Norris Bale's drive-way. She was short and dressed in a sharp suit under a thick, unzipped winter coat. The ends of her shiny bob were visible under a black, woolly hat. She opened her phone with a grim expression. I rolled down my window a touch to hear her words.

"Tell Swanson I've spoken to that neighbour. He's a miser-able son of a bitch."

She climbed into a MINI and slammed the door so I couldn't hear anything further. She must be a colleague of Swanson's. I hadn't thought of asking Norris if he'd seen anything. It was a long shot, but I didn't have any other options.

My hand shook as I knocked on Norris's door. The soft thud of footsteps from inside had me holding my breath. I didn't know what I was going to say or ask, but I had to try.

The door swung open, and his eyes narrowed suspiciously. His dishevelled hair and gruff expression made him look even more unpleasant in the dim light of the hallway.

"What is it now?" His voice was low, raspy.

"I need to ask you something," I began, the words coming out in a rush. "Have you seen anything unusual around here? Anyone hanging around my place? Or anything that doesn't seem right?"

He looked at me for a long moment. His eyes shifted uncomfortably before he let out a short, humourless laugh.

"It's your fault I had that awful policewoman around here asking me if I saw things, is it?" he snapped.

"The police have been round?" I asked, feigning innocence.

"Someone called them telling them to talk to me! You, I'm guessing? I should've known you were off your rocker. Your mother warned me you'd be trouble when you moved in. Said you had some issues. I didn't listen then, but I sure as hell

173

won't get involved now. No one's been hanging around except for you. I don't know what games you're playing, but I don't want any part of it."

I opened my mouth to argue but before I could say another word the door slammed shut in my face with a resounding thud. I stood there too stunned to move.

I looked down at the ground as I forced myself to walk back down his drive. I needed to gather my thoughts and decide what to do next. There was nothing left for me at the house. So I grabbed some extra clothes while it was daylight then headed back to the hotel.

My mind was grateful to have something to do other than worry on the drive over to the hotel. It wasn't too far away, so it only took a few minutes to reach it. I parked up close to the entrance in case I needed a quick getaway.

I made my way up the stairs rather than using the cramped lift, grateful to be away from the house at least.

But as I stepped into my room, I felt a cold breeze wash over my skin. I looked over at the window; it was open. Strange. I remembered closing it tightly before I left. Then my eyes fell on the bed, and I froze.

A letter waited for me on the pillow. The handwriting was unmistakable. My heart thundered in my chest as I clamped a hand over my mouth. He'd been here. He knew where I was.

I had nowhere left to hide.

The Shadow

Piper,

    You won't want to hear this because you always hated death, but it has to be him. He's living on borrowed time, always slipping through cracks, always one step ahead of the reckoning he deserves. But not anymore. I've made sure of that.

I've watched him long enough to know every lie he tells, every move he makes. The way he hides behind his charm, fooling everyone around him, pretending to be someone he's not. But I know him better than anyone. I know what he's done.

He deserves this. How many more lives would he ruin if I let him walk free? How many more chances would he steal from the people who actually deserve them?

No. It ends now.

It's not rage that drives me; it's clarity. The world will be better off without him in it. He's a problem that needs solving, a loose end that needs tying up. And I'm the only one who can do it.

It won't be easy. I know it won't. But, I've planned everything, every step, every moment. There's no escape for him this time. It's almost poetic, isn't it?

He always thought he was invincible. Untouchable. But he's not. He's just a man—a man who's about to face the consequences of everything he's done.

And when it's done, everything will be clear. You'll understand.

This is justice. This is balance.

You'll see.

Swanson

S wanson sat at the kitchen table, absentmindedly twirling a fork through the steam rising off his plate. The smell of roasted chicken and vegetables wafted through the air, but his appetite had disappeared days ago.

He couldn't stop thinking about Perry, who'd had a breakdown as soon as he and Summer reached the police station and had to be restrained and sent to hospital. Across from him, Summer was giving Joshua his plate of food.

"Eat up quickly, Joshua," she said. Her voice was light, though he knew she was as frustrated as he was about Perry. "Daddy will be here to pick you up for the weekend soon."

"Pasta, yes! Thanks, Mum," he replied as he grabbed a huge forkful of food.

Swanson glanced at his phone as it buzzed on the table beside him. The screen lit up with an incoming call from Piper Roberts. He hesitated before answering, his gut tightening.

"Piper?" he said as he swiped to answer. "What's going on?"

"Swanson, I'm terrified." Her voice came through panicked and shaky. "I've got another letter. It's saying someone is going to die, and I'm pretty sure it's about Adam. He's not answering his phone. I've tried calling him ten times. I don't know what to do. Please, Swanson, I think he's in danger."

"Piper, slow down." Swanson's grip on his phone tightened as he left the kitchen. "You said another letter? What exactly did it say?"

"I don't know how to explain it. It's vague, but it's threatening. Please, Swanson, you have to do something."

He glanced over at Summer, who felt his gaze and looked up. Her worried expression hardened when she saw the concern etched on his face.

"Where is Adam?"

"He's in Harrogate," Piper answered immediately. "I can send you his address. Please, I need help."

Swanson sighed, rubbing the back of his neck as he processed the information. Harrogate was a two-hour drive away. He wouldn't make it in time if Adam was already hurt.

"Alright," he said. "I'll call Harrogate station. Get someone to check on him. You've got his address?"

"I do," Piper confirmed, her voice a little calmer. "I'll text it to you and stay by the phone. Please let me know what happens."

"I'll let you know as soon as I hear anything," Swanson reassured her. "Try to stay calm. The local police will handle it. You don't need to worry."

Swanson hung up the phone. His mind raced with possibilities as he turned back to Summer. Maybe Adam was just sick of Piper's worrying and didn't want to pick up his phone.

"Sorry, I just need to make a call," he said, dialling the Harrogate police station as he spoke.

"Go ahead." Summer nodded. "I'll keep your dinner warm. Let me know if you need anything."

Swanson was on the phone for several minutes, giving the officer at the Harrogate station the details about Adam's address and Piper's concern. The officer assured him that someone would head out immediately to check on the address and confirm that everything was as it should be.

"I'll call you back with an update," the officer said before ending the call.

Swanson took a deep breath, trying to calm the nerves that were gnawing at him. All he could do was wait. And an hour later, just as he was helping Summer wash the dinner plates, his phone buzzed again.

"Swanson," the officer on the other end said quickly. "We've checked the address you gave us. Sad to say there's a body. It's a white male, early thirties, looks like he's been dead for a few hours."

"Is it Adam Bell?" Swanson's heart dropped.

"We're not sure yet," the officer said, their voice tight. "We've got the body at the scene. Forensics are on their way, but we're treating it as suspicious. I'll keep you posted as soon as we have more information."

Swanson hung up. He turned to Summer, who was standing by the sink watching him. She didn't need to ask what had happened. She could see it in his face.

"I need to call Piper," he told her.

"Of course," Summer replied quietly.

He quickly dialled Piper's number. It rang several times before she picked up. Her voice was strained as if she wasn't sure she wanted to hear what he had to say.

"Piper," he said, trying to keep his tone even. "The police were able to get to the address you gave me. Where are you? I'll come over if you're home."

"Just tell me, Swanson. Please. Spit it out."

He sighed, his hand tugged at his beard.

"There's a body. They're treating it as suspicious, but they haven't confirmed the identity yet."

"What do you mean they haven't confirmed it? Who is it?" Piper's voice was barely above a whisper.

"I don't know yet," Swanson said. "They're still working on it. I'll let you know when I hear anything more."

There was silence on the other end for a long moment. Swanson could hear Piper's shaky breath as she processed the news.

"Is it Adam?" she asked, her voice small.

"I don't know, Piper. I wish I had more answers. Just try to stay calm. I'll keep you updated. I know it's hard."

"I will. Please let me know as soon as you know something."

"Where are you? Do you have a friend you can call?"

"Yes, I'll call someone straight away."

Swanson finished the call and promised to keep her posted before hanging up. He turned back to Summer, who was watching him with a quiet, steady gaze. Joshua had left to get his shoes on before his dad arrived.

"I've just had a text from Hart asking me to make sure you call her," Summer said. "There was an emergency call made from the house next door to Piper's address. Norris Bale is dead."

Piper

I thought about driving to Harrogate to Adam's house, but what would have been the point? I had nowhere to go this time, not even a Pocket Stay Hotel. So I stayed in Derby to wait for more news and checked into a different hotel. I made sure no one followed me there. I kept my eye on the rearview mirror the whole time.

The new hotel was more expensive, though the bed was too soft and the room too quiet. The phone signal was rubbish. Every thought echoed in the stillness. Every sound, every memory. Every little thing reminded me of Adam.

I spent the night crying. I didn't even try to stop it. What was the point? I had been crying on and off for days since I found the first letter, and now after hearing that Adam was nowhere to be found and there's a body at his address. All I could do was lie there helpless, wishing it would all stop. But it didn't. It kept going. It kept getting worse.

It was Adam who'd kept me going. The thought of him moving in and of us having a baby together made me so happy. It would've been my very own little family. A proper family at last.

Unless the body wasn't his.

Hours passed and eventually, I couldn't sit in that hotel room any longer. I was drowning in my thoughts. My mind was too cluttered and my heart too heavy. I had to do something. Anything. Then I remembered Pinevale House.

I could go to work. Sue didn't know about Adam. She wouldn't ask questions about why I was there even though Adam was missing. I wasn't scheduled to work on a Saturday yet but I needed answers and I couldn't find them alone. If the body was Adam's, I needed justice for him. If it wasn't, I needed to save him before it was too late.

I had to know if any of the patients knew something that could explain the letters and what had happened. I had to make sure no one else was in danger. Maybe Lily knew something. Maybe she saw something that night when she was peering out of the window.

So I got up and got dressed in a rush. I barely registered what I was wearing. My reflection in the hotel mirror showed someone I didn't recognise. The bags under my eyes were enormous.

I realised halfway through getting ready that I'd left my work T-shirt at home. Cursing under my breath, I grabbed my car keys and swung by my house before heading to Pinevale. The last thing I needed to deal with Sue's judgmental looks for showing up out of uniform.

But my heart sank as I turned onto my street. Police cars parked all along the pavement. Their lights flashed silently in the grey morning. Officers clustered around Norris Bale's house, their expressions grim. A wave of unease swept over me as I slowed the car. I craned my neck, trying to see what was going on, but I couldn't make anything out.

I tightened my grip on the steering wheel. Whatever was happening, I didn't have time to get involved. Maybe it was coincidental. It might not even be related to my note leaving stalker. Unless Norris was the one leaving letters and they were arresting him. I almost laughed at the thought of him having any interest in me.

I pulled out my phone to check if Swanson had got back to me. I cursed when I saw three missed calls and a voicemail. The signal must have been worse than I realised inside the new hotel. I brought the phone up to my ear and listened to the new voicemail with bated breath.

'Piper, it's Alex Swanson. I don't have an identity of the body yet, but please don't go home tonight. Stay with your friend.'

I breathed a sigh of relief. They hadn't identified Adam yet. He might still be alive. I tried calling Swanson's phone again, but it went straight to voicemail.

Fuck it. I didn't have time to waste worrying about Norris bloody Bale and what might have happened to him. I hit the pedal and kept going, leaving the scene behind me. Work would have to do without my uniform.

But as I made my way to Pinevale House, I couldn't help thinking about Norris. After I'd parked up on the driveway rather than the road, I rang Swanson back. He didn't answer. So I shot him a quick text message asking what had happened at Norris Bale's house. When I walked inside, I walked straight into Sue. She looked me up and down, her mouth dropped open.

"Piper!" she said, almost looking concerned. "You look awful. What happened to you?"

"I'm fine," I said quickly, forcing a smile. "Just tired."

"Did he get to you?" she asked, eyes wide.

My stomach clenched. Who the hell was she talking about?

"Did who get to me?"

Her gaze shifted to the door, as if she said something wrong and was about to run away.

"The, um, the letter writer. Who else?"

"Oh!" I really was seeing signs where there weren't any. "No. I'm just tired."

"You know you're not scheduled to work today, right?"

"Yes. I felt bad for being off sick in my first week. You don't have to pay me, but I wanted to make up for it and keep learning."

"Well, that's fine. But try to pull yourself together." She didn't look convinced, but I was grateful she didn't push. "The patients won't like seeing you like this."

I nodded, but I wasn't listening. My mind was already on Adam. I had to start with Lily. She was the one who had been watching the car park. She noticed things others didn't.

I found her in the corner of the living room wrapped up in a blanket. She was sitting in one of the worn chairs with her legs pulled up to her chest. Her drawing pad was in front of her, and she was scribbling away as usual.

She didn't notice me at first. I almost didn't want to interrupt her. She looked so peaceful for once; it was nice to see. Everything in me would have loved to wrap her up in a nice warm coat and bring her home with me to look after. I approached her slowly.

"Lily?"

She stopped scribbling. Her wary gaze flickered up at me.

"Hi, Piper," she mumbled.

Despite her youth, there was something about her that made her seem so much older. Her eyes were hollow, like she'd seen more than anyone should have to.

"I need to ask you something," I began, sitting down across from her. "About Monday evening when you were looking out the window and I was leaving. Did you see anyone?"

Lily's face went even paler and she shifted in her seat, glancing around nervously. I could feel her hesitance. Discomfort radiated off of her. I couldn't push too hard, but I had to try.

"It's okay," I said gently, trying to soften my voice. "I just need to know what you saw. It could help someone. Me, mainly."

She swallowed hard, like the thought of speaking about what she saw made her anxious. She fiddled with her drawing pad and then turned the pages to an older drawing.

"I saw a man," she whispered as she passed me the picture.

It was the one I saw her drawing on Tuesday morning. I recognised the chaotic lines that now made the outline of a figure dressed in black trousers and a black hoodie.

"I didn't see his face, but he was tall and white skinned. He left something on your car."

"What was it?" I asked, hoping she'd confirm it was a letter she saw.

"I don't know. I couldn't see properly," Lily said. Her fingers twisted around the fabric of her blanket. "I just saw him put something down. It was dark out, and I was far away, so I couldn't really see what it was. But he was acting strange, like he was waiting for something."

"You're sure that's all you remember?" I pressed. I could already see she was trying to pull away into herself again.

"Yeah." Lily nodded slowly. "He didn't notice me, but I saw him. I think he was watching you."

My stomach twisted. This was proof I wasn't going crazy. There really was someone out there watching me.

I noticed the pale skin of Lily's arms. She'd hidden most of her wrist under the sleeve of her jumper, but I could see the faint outlines of scars on the skin that peeked out. They were the telltale signs of self-harm. It was like looking in a mirror.

I knew it was unprofessional, but something about the shared pain made me feel the need to connect. So I rolled up my sleeve and showed her my wrist. Not the one damaged by the fire, but the one I damaged myself when I was eighteen. The same place I'd damaged the little bear by slicing right through him. The marks had faded but were still visible, and she gasped with wide eyes.

"I know what it's like," I whispered. "I know how it feels."

"I know I'm not supposed to, but I cut sometimes too," she muttered, her voice a little steadier than before. "When it gets too much."

"Next time, use your rubber band or come find me or Sue," I told her, and she nodded. "Do you remember anything else about the man, Lily? Anything at all?"

"No. I couldn't see much. Just that he was tall and wore black. He was just standing there staring at the house, and then he got into a car when he saw you leave."

"A car? What kind of car?"

She shrugged. "A red one."

"Did you get the plate?"

"No." She looked down at her lap, her face crumpling slightly. "It was too dark."

I nodded, my chest tight.

"Thank you, Lily. I know this is hard, but you've helped me so much."

"I know something else, too."

"What?"

"Peter didn't come home last night."

"Where is he?"

"I don't know. Keep the drawing," she said as she pushed the paper into my hand.

"Lily, why were you watching the car park? Is it because of Peter? You can tell me. I'll help you. So will Sue."

She takes a shaky breath, and nods so subtly I can barely see it.

"Shall we talk to Sue?"

"You can, but don't mention my name to her, please?"

I sigh. "I can't promise anything, Lily. If he's been doing things he shouldn't be doing, then your name might need to be mentioned. But we'll see."

I walked away staring at the drawing. The chaotic lines of the man's figure seemed to swirl into a shape near his hand. A set of keys? A knife? I couldn't tell, but the thought made my stomach churn.

Lily had helped me more than she'd ever realise. Her story was proof that he was real. I wasn't losing my mind.

Relief fought against the dread that tightened my chest. I wasn't imagining things. I wasn't crazy. But that relief was short-lived, swallowed by the question that gnawed at me. Why me? Why Adam?

Standing by the staff room door, I glanced at my trembling hands. This wasn't over. I needed to stay ahead of him. Because if I didn't, I'd never see the next move coming. Clenching my fists, I pushed open the door and made my way to the office. It was time to piece this puzzle together before it consumed me entirely. And first on my list were Sue and Peter.

Piper

Sue told me to leave the home half an hour later. She'd called the police to discuss Peter's disappearance and what he might have done to Lily, and they were on their way, but she looked genuinely worried about me and told me to be careful.

I couldn't bring myself to go back to the hotel. The cramped room and quiet walls were suffocating, and the thin chain lock on the door didn't exactly scream safety. I had to go back home. I needed answers, and the letter writer always knew where I was, anyway. Hiding was pointless.

The drive home was a blur. My head throbbed with questions. None of which made sense. There was also the faint hope that I might find something that could explain all this madness, and that was the only thing keeping me going. As well as praying the body was not Adam and we would get our happy ending at last.

The house loomed dark and silent when I arrived. The police had left Norris Bale's premises but the police tape still ran around his house. Swanson had not replied to my text message. So I swallowed hard and let myself in and locked the door behind me. My fingers trembled as they turned the bolt.

Then I tore through the house room by room searching for

something. I didn't even know what. More letters? Photos? Some clue why my life was unravelling?

I emptied drawers onto the floor, yanked the wardrobes open, and rifled through every cupboard. By the time I made it to the attic, sweat clung to my skin despite the chill in the air. I pulled the rickety ladder down and climbed up the old wooden steps, which creaked beneath my feet.

Dust swirled in the air as I reached the top and stepped onto uneven floorboards. It was pitch black up there, and I fumbled for the pull string on the single bulb.

The light flickered to life and cast shadows across the cluttered space. My breath hitched as I scanned the room. There were boxes of my parents' forgotten belongings everywhere. And then I saw them.

Footprints.

Large footprints pressed into a thick layer of dust and leading across the attic floor. They weren't mine. They couldn't be mine. They were too big. My legs froze, refusing to take another step. Someone had been here. He had been here. This is probably where he'd hidden when monitoring me.

My stomach churned violently as bile rose in my throat. The edges of my vision blurred as panic clawed its way through me. I stumbled back down the ladder, barely making it to the bathroom before I threw up into the sink.

I gripped the edge of the counter. My stomach clenched again, but it wasn't from fear this time. A strange thought wormed its way into my head, something I hadn't considered until now.

I hadn't had a period since before Evelyn's funeral.

The thought sent a fresh wave of nausea crashing over me. I grabbed my keys and bolted out of the house, my heart racing as I drove to the nearest supermarket. My hands were shaking so badly when I grabbed the pregnancy test I dropped it twice before making it to the self-checkout.

The fluorescent lights in the supermarket bathroom were harsh, making everything feel more surreal. I locked myself in the stall, my breaths shallow as I ripped the box open and fumbled with the test.

The seconds stretched into an eternity as I waited for the result. I told myself it couldn't be true. Not now. Not with everything falling apart. But when I looked down, my worst fear—and my greatest hope—was staring back at me.

Two lines.

Positive.

* * *

I went straight home, unsure what else to do. Then the knock at the door came just as I sank onto the sofa with exhaustion pulling at every muscle in my body. I froze. No one ever came here unannounced since I'd moved back. Then another knock came, firmer this time.

"Piper, it's DI Swanson," came the familiar voice.

I dragged myself back up and opened the door to find Swanson standing there. His broad frame filled the doorway. He wasn't alone. Beside him was a petite woman with cropped, brown hair and sharp eyes that seemed to miss nothing. She had the air of someone who didn't take nonsense from anyone, her expression cool but professional.

"Piper," Swanson said, his tone low. "This is DI Rebecca Hart. She works with me."

"Sorry for the intrusion." Hart gave a quick nod. "But we thought it would be better to do this in person."

Her voice was brisk, but there was a faint softness to it, like she was trying not to make things worse.

"I texted you ages ago," I said to Swanson.

"I know. My apologies. I've been dealing with something urgent."

"Norris Bale? What happened?"

"Someone shot him," Hart replied.

My mouth dropped open. I couldn't form a response, so silently stepped aside to let them in. My stomach tightened as they entered. Someone *shot* Norris? Another shooting? They were definitely going to think it was me. I suddenly wanted to kick them back out.

Swanson moved with a deliberate calm with his hands in his pockets, while Hart scanned the room. "He's dead?" I asked.

"Yes." Swanson glanced at Hart. "I'm afraid your neighbour died from his wound. Someone shot him in the head."

"Is that what you're here to tell me?"

"No."

"Have a seat," I said, my voice quieter than I'd intended.

Swanson and Hart sat across from me at the small kitchen table. Something gentler tempered Swanson's usual gruffness, but Hart's gaze stayed locked on me like she was trying to figure me out.

"What's this about then if not Norris Bale?" I asked, as though the answer wasn't obvious.

Swanson cleared his throat. I held my breath, trying to steel myself to hear bad news about the only man I'd ever loved. The man whose little baby was growing inside me as we spoke.

"We've identified the body found in Harrogate using the ID found at the scene." He paused, his eyes meeting mine. "It's Adam. I'm sorry, Piper."

I felt the words hit me like a punch to the gut. Adam. He was really gone. I expected pain and tears, but I only felt numbness. Though it was suddenly much harder to breathe. When I remained silent, Swanson continued in his steady voice.

"It was quick. They shot him from the back. He didn't suffer. We're still piecing things together, but it looks like someone directly targeted him."

The room seemed to shrink. The walls closed in as I tried to process what he was saying. Shot. Targeted. Just like Norris and Evelyn. Just like my parents. My head spun, and I gripped the edge of the table to steady myself.

Hart spoke then, her voice cutting through the fog in my mind.

"I know this is a lot to take in, but we need to ask if Adam mentioned anything unusual before this happened. Any threats, anyone he was worried about?"

I shook my head numbly.

"No. He said nothing like that." My voice cracked, and I cleared my throat, trying to hold it together. "It was only me receiving threats."

"Do you know if Adam had a family in Harrogate who could help with identification or next steps?" Swanson leaned forward, his tone softer now.

"No," I whispered, shaking my head again. "He talked little about his family. He always said I was his only family now."

Swanson nodded, his expression thoughtful. Hart stayed silent as her sharp eyes flicked between us. I felt the tears burn behind my eyes, but I blinked them back. I couldn't fall apart now. Not in front of them. Not when there were still so many questions.

"Do you have any leads on the letters?" I asked, my voice

stronger than I expected.

"Not yet." Swanson's expression darkened slightly. "That's part of why we're here. Dr Summer Thomas, our psychologist, is speaking with the Pinevale House psychiatrist to see which patients we can interview about the letters. We want to see if any of them might have been involved."

"A patient called Lily told me she saw a man," I said. I rummaged in the handbag sitting on the table in front of me. "Here. She drew this. She also said he got into a red car."

I passed Swanson the paper Lily had given me. But my focus had already shifted. This psycho had shot Adam. My Adam. My mind was racing. I thought of the footprints in the attic, the letters, and Michael Grey. It had to be him. It all fit. Except for the handwriting being so much like my father's. Maybe that was a coincidence.

But Swanson didn't need to hear my suspicions. Not yet. I wasn't ready to share that part of the story, not until I had more answers. Not until I knew what I wanted to do about it.

"I need some air," I said abruptly, standing up.

"Piper," Swanson began, but I shook my head.

"Thank you for coming. Really. But I need a minute and I want to be on my own."

Swanson exchanged a glance with Hart, who nodded subtly. They stood. Swanson placed a hand on the back of the chair as if he wasn't sure whether to leave or stay.

"Call me if you need anything," he said finally. "Take care of yourself."

I nodded, not trusting myself to speak. As they left, I stood in the doorway and watched their car pull away until the sound of the engine fading into the distance. Slowly, I returned to the sofa. My body ached with exhaustion. I reached for another bottle of wine and twisted the cap off before realising I couldn't drink anymore. A sharp curse escaped my lips as I threw the bottle into the bin. The clatter echoed in the silent room.

That's when the tears finally came. I collapsed onto the sofa, my chest heaving as raw grief poured out of me relentlessly. Adam was gone. I'd lost the only man I'd ever loved.

I don't know how long I cried, but the feeling inside me felt unbearable. Yet amidst the grief, something else rose. It started as a flicker and grew steadily stronger. Resolve.

I would find Michael Grey, and I would make him pay for what he'd done.

That was the last thought I remember as exhaustion finally overtook me. I drifted into sleep clutching the pillow like a teddy bear.

There was no fire in my dreams, but there was a memory lost within it. A memory of feeling this grief once before. Of missing someone I loved more than anything on this earth. Someone lost in the shadows that I couldn't quite see.

When I awoke Sunday morning, my eyes were heavier than I'd ever felt them. It took a moment to remember that Adam was gone, and the ache in my chest returned tenfold. I reached out to stroke my chest, as if rubbing it could make the pain go away. It wasn't until I raised my other hand I realised something was in it.

Another letter.

This time placed right into my hand as I slept.

The Shadow

Dear Piper,

You've been so busy lately, haven't you? Rushing around, digging into things. But you're doing so well, even if you're a little off track. I forgive you. I always do. Don't cry. It will all be okay. I promise.

And now, I see that you've been hiding something wonderful for us to share.

You're glowing, Piper. Did you know that? I noticed it when you didn't think anyone else would. The way your hand lingers on your stomach, as if you're already protecting what's inside. It's beautiful. You're beautiful. They will be beautiful.

I couldn't be happier for us. This is what we deserve. It's a fresh start. Something new to hold on to. Someone to love unconditionally. I'll keep you safe, Piper. I'll keep both of you safe. No one will ever tear us apart again.

It's nearly time. Everything's falling into place now, just like it's meant to. Don't worry and don't be sad anymore, you'll see me soon.

We'll be together. All of us.

You'll see.

Piper

My stomach lurched, and I ran to the kitchen sink to throw up. The terror was so strong I couldn't even cry. He'd been standing right over me and I hadn't even woken.

And he knew about the baby.

The thought of the baby spurred me into action. I needed to find Michael Grey, and I needed to do it now. The police were not moving quickly enough, and now Evelyn, Norris and Adam were all dead and I could be next.

Nottingham Psychiatric Hospital wasn't far, and I spent the drive rehearsing every detail of my story. I knew how to play this game. I'd done it before. My old job as a bank agency support worker gave me more than enough insider knowledge to sound convincing. I turned up to different hospitals all the time when they needed an extra member of staff. Most of the time they didn't double check who I was. All I needed was a little luck. Which in fairness, had been in short supply lately.

The hospital loomed ahead, its grey facade as cold and uninviting as I'd imagined. I parked around the corner and walked in to the front doors. I forced my hands to stay steady as I adjusted my coat and strode toward the reception desk.

"Can I help you?" The receptionist looked up, her expression pinched and tired. Her hair, pulled into a tight bun, was peppered with grey streaks, and the dark circles under her eyes suggested she'd been there far longer than her shift demanded.

"Hi, I'm from the bank staff. Here to cover a shift." I showed her my old ID that I'd never handed back. It still lived in the bottom of my handbag with years old receipts.

"I wasn't told about this." Her brows furrowed, and she tapped her pen against the desk.

"Oh, sorry." I shrugged lightly, keeping my tone casual. "I think it was a last-minute thing."

She hesitated, glancing at the phone as if she might call someone but then shook her head.

"No one ever tells me anything around here, anyway. Go on through."

I felt the tension in my chest loosen as I nodded gratefully and stepped past the desk, making my way toward the airlock that led to the main male ward.

The hospital was oppressive. Inside was a maze of sterile, white walls and fluorescent lights, and the smell of disinfectant hung in the air. Occasional muffled voices echoed through the corridors from the side rooms, which included a small gym and a computer room. All of them were locked.

I found the ward easily enough. The sign above the door read Male Rehabilitation: Ruby Ward. The locked door's reinforced glass revealed a younger male staff member walking around with a clipboard in hand. He moved quickly, his expression focused but not unkind. I pressed the buzzer and waited as his eyes flicked towards me. He must have been in his late twenties like me, with short, dark hair and a skinny frame. He approached the door and opened it, leaning out slightly. His scrubs were slightly wrinkled, and he had the relaxed demeanour of someone who was used to chaos.

"Hi, can I help?" he asked with a smile.

"I'm one of the bank staff here to cover a shift." I smiled back. "Piper."

"Oh, hey. I'm Darren," he replied without an ounce of suspicion. "Do you need me to show you around?"

"No, thank you," I answered brightly. "I've been here a few times. I'll just go put some things in the nurses' station."

He nodded and walked away. I quickly scanned the area. The walls were a uniform shade of magnolia, their blankness occasionally interrupted by faded posters reminding staff about hand hygiene and mental health awareness. Mismatched chairs and a worn sofa dotted the common area in front of me. Its fabric had faded from years of use.

Then I spotted a nurses' station across the ward. In wards like this, the stations were typically small, locked rooms with reinforced glass windows offering a clear view of the patients, and Ruby Ward was no different.

I made my way over, glancing at the patients milling around as I approached. Most were subdued. Their movements were slow and unhurried. None of them even looked at me. The door to the station was firmly closed, and fingerprints smudged the window. Inside the room, a pretty, young nurse sat tapping away at the computer. The orange light of the computer screen reflected on her glasses.

I knocked gently on the glass, and she looked up. Her face brightened with a welcoming smile when she spotted me. She stood and unlocked the door.

"Hi there, come on in," she said warmly as she stepped aside to let me enter. "Are you bank staff?"

"Yes." I walked in with feigned frustration. "I was on the

other ward but they've sent me over here. Are you logged in already? I just need to write up some notes."

She barely glanced at me before sliding the keyboard towards me.

"Yeah, sure. Here you go." She exited the room and left me to it, uninterested in what I was doing.

"Thanks," I muttered, my fingers already flying across the keys as I pulled up the patient database. This hospital used the same database system as I had used in Harrogate Hospital as they were both NHS, so I had no trouble accessing the information.

My heart pounded as I typed in Michael Grey's name. The loading bar felt like it stretched on forever, each second tightening the coil of tension in my chest. And then, there it was.

'Michael Grey. Status: Transferred.'

My stomach dropped as I scrolled through the notes. They'd discharged him weeks ago. His file was marked with a request to move to Woodview, an open mental health home in Derbyshire. The notes listed the new address, and I recognised the location immediately.

It was right near my house.

I couldn't breathe. The walls of the hospital seemed to close in around me as I jotted down the address. My hands trembled as I tried to write. He'd been so close to me this whole time.

I made an excuse about needing to make a phone call and left the ward. And just as quickly exited the hospital. The receptionist was confused when I ran past her, but I barely noticed her response. My mind raced as I drove back towards Derby and thoughts of Michael Grey consumed me.

Was he the one behind the letters? The one who had taken

Adam from me? The pieces didn't fit perfectly, but the edges were aligning.

Woodview was a nondescript house and was smaller than Oakleigh or Pinevale. It couldn't have been more than a four-bedroomed home, and it blended into the quiet residential street like it belonged there. It looked the same as any other property except with a larger driveway and more cars parked on it.

I'd seen Michael Grey before. There was no trial because he confessed. But I'd seen him in court as he admitted what he did. He'd shown no remorse. He was a hunched over, harmless looking man who'd be about thirty-five years old now. My relationship with my parents might have been strained, but that bastard had taken away any chance of us being able to make amends.

I was pregnant and alone because of him.

I parked a little way down the street and waited, my heart pounding so hard it drowned out every other sound. The minutes stretched into an hour, and the sky deepened into a thick black. I clenched the steering wheel. Just as I was about to give up, the door creaked open.

I sat up straighter, my breath catching in my throat. A shadow moved across the doorway and stepped out onto the porch. My stomach dropped so fast I thought I might be sick.

This man wasn't small or frail. He didn't move like someone afraid of being caught. He was tall. Confident

Familiar. The world tilted. This man was not Michael Grey.

It was Adam.

He was alive, and standing right in front of me like he hadn't just died.

He looked different, but it was him. I couldn't believe what I was seeing. My hands gripped the steering wheel as I watched him walk down the driveway and disappear into a red car. He turned on the engine and drove the opposite way.

I wanted to follow and scream and demand answers, but I couldn't move. My mind whirled, torn between relief and fear.

I couldn't breathe. Adam wasn't dead, and I wasn't sure what was more confusing. That he was actually still alive, or that I suddenly wasn't sure I wanted to find him.

But if he wasn't dead, then what the hell was going on?

My hands shook so badly on the drive back home that I had to pull over twice just to calm myself down. My gravity had shifted, and nothing made sense anymore. Adam was alive.

Adam, who I loved, who I trusted.

The man who had lied to me.

The man whose baby I carried.

My thoughts churned, looping through the same questions with no answers. Was he behind the letters? Was he playing some kind of sick game? Why had the police found a body someone claimed was his?

I barely registered parking the car as I reached home or when I stepped inside. My movements were mechanical as if my body was working on autopilot. Inside, the silence pressed down on me. I leaned against the door, closing my eyes and trying to steady my breath. But the images kept flashing in my mind of Adam walking out of that house, alive and well. Yet somehow, looking like a stranger.

Just like Dad had.

Is that what was happening again? I paced the living room. Should I call the police? Tell them what I saw? Swanson would listen, wouldn't he? He'd believe me.

But the thought of explaining this to anyone made my

stomach turn. He might think I was crazy. I couldn't call them. Not yet.

I grabbed a glass of water from the kitchen, gulping it down as I tried to think. Something needed to be done. I couldn't just sit here waiting for him to come back into my life on his terms. If Adam was behind this, if he was the one who'd been sending the letters and leading me to spiral, I needed answers.

The idea hit me so suddenly it almost startled me.

I grabbed a pen and a piece of paper. My hands were clammy as I scribbled down the words.

Adam,

I know. I saw you, and I understand now. Let's talk. Meet me at the house for dinner. You know where I am. Let's end this.

Your love,

Piper

The edges of the paper trembled as I folded it up. It wasn't perfect but it would do. If he was watching me like I thought he was, he'd see it. He'd come.

I placed the note on the windscreen of my car and anchored it with the wiper. Then I stood there for a moment, staring at it as my stomach twisted with nerves.

Was this the right move or was I making a huge mistake?

I didn't know. Everything felt like a gamble. But one thing was certain. I would not sit around waiting for answers. I was done with waiting.

It wasn't long before there was a noise at my front door, and another white envelope slipped through my letterbox.

The Shadow

Dear Piper,

 I knew you'd figure it out. You're clever like that. So much sharper than people give you credit for. And now, finally, you've left me something. A sign. An invitation.

I can't tell you how happy this makes me. You've been so brave through all of this, pushing forward even when the odds were stacked against you.

I knew you would be. That's the Piper I know.

You've made the right choice, leaving me that note. We've been dancing around this for so long, haven't we? And now, the time has come. But don't fight this, Piper.

No more guessing, no more waiting. Tonight, we'll see each other, and everything will fall into place.

At 6 PM, Piper. That's when it begins.

I imagine your heart is racing right now, Piper. It should be. It's almost time. Be ready. This is the moment we've both been waiting for since the fire.

I've waited long enough to hold what's mine. We'll finally be together.

Just as it was always meant to be before she made me go away.

You'll see.

Swanson

The sterile scent hit Swanson as he walked through the doors of the hospital with Hart by his side. The corridor was quiet. Their walls were lined with muted colours meant to soothe the mind, but it did nothing for the knot in Swanson's chest. Perry Vance was in the psychiatric ward of Derby Royal Hospital after his breakdown, and they were hoping he'd finally give them something useful.

"Think he'll talk?" Hart glanced at Swanson as they approached the ward.

"At least two people are dead, and another one is missing. If he knows something, we need to make sure he talks." Swanson shrugged. "Let's hope he trusts us enough without Summer with us."

After two people being shot dead already, Swanson wasn't allowing Summer anywhere near the case again. When they reached the ward, the nurse on duty waved them through to a private room. They found Perry sitting on the edge of his bed. His hands fidgeted in his lap. He looked up as they entered. Exhaustion shadowed his wide eyes.

"Perry," Swanson said, keeping his voice calm. "Thanks for letting us speak with you."

"I had no choice, did I?" Perry said, his gaze moving between

Swanson and Hart.

"No," Hart said bluntly, pulling out a chair and sitting down across from him. "But you have a choice about what you tell us. We need the truth, Perry."

"I've already said too much." Perry swallowed hard, his Adam's apple bobbing.

Swanson took the seat beside Hart and leaned forward slightly.

"No one's here to hurt you. We're just trying to piece things together. You're not in trouble, but we haven't found Hayley Smith, and we think you know something that could help us find her."

Perry's fingers twisted together. He glanced at the door like he wanted to bolt, but there was no way to reach it without trying to get past both of them. Swanson's size might make him look like the muscle, but even he would never want to go face to face with Rebecca Hart.

"I think I know who took her. I think it was Michael," he whispered after a long pause.

"Michael Grey?" Swanson pressed gently.

"How did you know?" Perry's head snapped up, his eyes wide with fear. "Oh god, he's going to kill me."

"No one is going to hurt you, Perry." Hart leaned forward, her expression firm but empathetic. "Grey can't touch you here. But we can't protect you if we don't know what's going on. Tell us about Michael."

Perry hesitated. He glanced at the door again. His lower lip trembled, and then he finally broke down.

"I met him at the local pub. It wasn't long after I moved out of Oakleigh Home. It scared me, you know? Being on my own for the first time in years. But Michael said he understood.

205

He'd just left a place himself, and he said he'd look after me."

"How did he 'look after' you?" Swanson's brow furrowed.

"At first he was nice." Perry's gaze fell to the floor. "He said I could trust him and he even stayed at my place sometimes during the day. He said he needed somewhere quiet. Somewhere away from people. And he used my computer."

"What was he using it for?" Hart tilted her head.

"I don't know," Perry stammered, his voice rising as he looked back up at her. "He wouldn't let me look. He said it was private. That it wasn't my business. I didn't want to make him mad. I don't like it when people are mad at me."

"Did anyone else know about Michael staying at your house?" Swanson's jaw tightened.

Perry nodded slowly, his gaze dropping to the floor again.

"Hayley knew. She came over one day unannounced. She wasn't supposed to. I guess she was worried about me because she said I'd been rushing her out during her normal visits. She saw something she wasn't supposed to see."

"Perry," Hart said firmly. "What did she see?"

"She saw what Michael was doing on the computer," Perry whispered, his voice barely audible. "There were videos of a woman. I didn't see them, but Hayley did. I heard what she said to him. She freaked out. She said she was going to call the police."

"And what did Michael do?" Swanson exchanged a sharp glance with Hart.

"He told her to calm down," Perry said, his breathing quickening. "But she wouldn't listen. She stormed out, and he made me promise not to say anything. He said if I told anyone about him or Hayley then he'd make me sorry. Then he said I needed to help him with some things."

"What things?" Hart asked.

"To help make sure no one knew about him."

"Is that why you called Summer Thomas?" Swanson's fists clenched under the table. "Did Michael make you do that?"

Perry nodded miserably.

"How did he know her number?"

"Michael had it. He said it wasn't hard to find. She used to be an advocate back at his hospital. He heard staff saying she was going to work for the police and that calling her was a distraction for you. That it would keep people off his trail. He told me what to say the first time. He doesn't know I called her the second time. I was trying to help."

"Have you told anyone else about this?" Hart asked.

"No." He shook his head. "But I tried to warn Piper once."

"So you know who Piper is?" Swanson asked.

"I didn't. I heard Michael talking to someone called Piper when he was at mine a few times. I think she was the woman on the computer. That was just a guess at first. Then I followed Michael once to see what he was doing. I saw her. She's very pretty. I didn't want him to hurt her, too."

"Did you speak to her?" Swanson asked.

"No. I wanted to. I knocked on her door the next day. Then I realised his red car was outside and ran away."

"Do you know where Michael is now?" Hart leaned back in her chair, her expression hard.

"I haven't seen him for a few days." Perry shook his head. Tears brimmed in his eyes. "I swear I didn't know what he was planning. I didn't know he'd hurt Hayley. Before she went missing, I thought he was just going to run away."

"We believe you," Swanson said. "But you need to help us, Perry. Anything you can tell us about Michael, anything you remember, could be the key to stopping him."

"He's still watching her." Perry wiped his eyes with the back of his hand. "He talks about her like he loved her."

Swanson's stomach sank. He needed to find Piper.

"We need to move. Now," Hart snapped, clearly feeling the same way.

"We'll find him," Swanson said firmly, rising to his feet. "You've done the right thing by telling us, Perry. You're safe now."

As they left the room, Hart glanced at Swanson, her jaw tight.

"We're finally getting somewhere," she said.

Swanson nodded as his phone rang. He removed it from his pocket and pulled a face at the screen. It was Pinevale House.

"Swanson," he answered sharply.

"Be quick," Hart mouthed. He shooed her and turned to face the other way.

"Hi, my name is Sue Blake." Her words were brisk. "I'm the manager at Pinevale. You gave me your number to help organise the patient interviews."

"Yes, I remember. How can I help?"

"It's Piper. I should have said something before, but I was so scared."

She sighed heavily. Swanson turned back to Hart, who was tapping her foot with her arms crossed against her chest. But she stopped when she saw his face.

"It's Sue," he mouthed as he placed the call on speaker.

Sue made a noise that sounded like a sob.

"Go on, Sue. It's okay. You can tell me."

"I had a call a few weeks ago, before she came to work here. I didn't know the voice, but it was from a man. He told me to make sure I interviewed her or I'd be sorry. I assumed it was her partner. I laughed it off, told him to leave me alone but—"

She sobbed again, and Swanson gave her a second to compose herself.

"Please, Sue. I think Piper is in danger. Anything you can tell us would be useful."

"Well, that night he broke into my house. He wore a mask so I couldn't see what he looked like. I live alone with my fifteen-year-old daughter, and he threatened to hurt her if I didn't employ Piper. So I did."

"You didn't call the police?"

"I just wanted to keep my daughter safe. Her father died of cancer six months ago and she's been through so much."

"I'm sorry, Sue."

"Since his death, my head hasn't been screwed on right. If I'm honest, after the interview I thought Piper would be great and maybe I could help her get away from this crazy guy or maybe the whole thing would just go away."

"You could've said something when we asked about the letters," Swanson replied.

"I know." She sobbed again. "I just freaked out."

"Why tell us now?"

"My daughter and I are away. Peter's gone missing. I've told the police about him already but a different officer visited to get my statement. We're staying with my mother for a week so I can keep us safe. Please, find this guy before we have to go home, and make sure my daughter and Piper are safe."

"Text me your mother's address. I'll send an officer round shortly to take your statement about this, too. They'll want to know everything. Dates, his accent, type of mask, anything that could help. Let me know if you think of anything else important like where he might be. Call me directly."

He hung up quickly. It seemed like simple Michael Grey was far more dangerous than anyone had given him credit for. He was always five steps ahead. And he's already trapped Piper in his game. The only question now was whether they'd reach her in time.

Piper

The next hour ticked by slowly. Each second dragged as I tried to distract myself. Swanson kept trying to call, and even turned up at the house once, but I didn't answer or respond. I was sick of the police pretending to help. He could wait. I paced the house, tidying and straightening things that didn't need it, but nothing could stop the storm of nerves in my chest.

Adam was coming.

Maybe I should've been more scared, but how could I fear someone I loved so much? This was a man who had never hurt me. Adam did *not* kill anybody. Whatever was going on, he could not be the one who was responsible for the deaths.

I cooked dinner to win him over and show him I was still on his side. I set the table and pulled out the nicer plates that Mum had always saved for special occasions. It felt surreal, like I was preparing for a fun first date instead of whatever this was going to turn out to be.

I opened the fridge and pulled out what I could to make his favourite dinner. The contents of my fridge and cupboards were sparse. Though I found some chicken, garlic, and stock. I added salt, pepper, onion, and chives. The rice went in last and I stirred it continuously before adding cream. Cooking kept my hands busy but not my mind. What was I even going to say? How could I possibly make sense of all this?

By the time six p.m. rolled around, my heart felt like it was going to burst out of my chest. I kept glancing at the clock, then at the door, waiting for the knock that would confirm I hadn't imagined all of it. And then it came.

The knock was sudden despite my expectation. My legs felt like jelly as I made my way to the door and gripped the handle tightly. I opened it, and there he was.

Adam.

I choked back a sob and trembled with emotion. It was really him. He was somehow taller than I remembered. His shoulders seemed broader, and his face harder. There was something different about him, like he'd shed whatever softness he used to have, and he no longer slouched.

But I didn't care. I burst into tears and threw my arms around the man I loved. The man I'd thought was dead earlier today. It was the best feeling in the world to have his arms wrapped around me once more. Even though he smelled different.

"Adam," I whispered as I pulled back. "You're alive."

His lips curved into a small smile, but his eyes glinted.

"Piper," he said. His voice was almost the same. Yet it was a breath slower. Like someone wearing his skin and trying to get the rhythm right. "You finally figured it out."

I still couldn't move. My mind reeled as I took him in, alive and standing in front of me when he wasn't supposed to be.

"I missed you," he said, stepping closer. His presence filled the doorway, overwhelming and intoxicating all at once. "I hated being away from you."

"Adam," I said again, my voice cracking. "What is going on? They said you were dead."

He raised a hand and gently cupped my cheek. The warmth of the touch I never thought I'd feel again sent a jolt through me.

"Later," he breathed. "Let's eat first. I'm starving."

Before I could protest, he leaned in and kissed me. His lips were firm and demanding against mine. It wasn't like before, not the way I remembered. This was different. He was more intense. More dominant. I pulled back, breathless and confused.

"Dinner," I stammered. "Right, dinner."

He followed me inside, his eyes scanning the room as if he hadn't seen it before.

"Risotto," he said, glancing at the table and the food waiting for him. "My favourite."

I nodded, watching as he sat down. He was completely at ease while I felt like a stranger in my own home.

We ate almost in silence. I found the tension in the air unbearable. He seemed completely calm, almost amused, while I could barely keep my hands steady. When I'd cleared the plates, he stood and crossed the room to where I was by the sink.

"Piper," he said, his voice more commanding than I was used to. "Come here."

I don't know what possessed me, but I stepped closer and he pulled me into his arms. His mouth crashed against mine with a force I'd never felt.

This wasn't the Adam I knew. He was so much more sure of himself. But the way he touched me, the way his hands moved over my body, ignited something deep inside me. Something I had never felt.

A tiny alarm bell rang in the back of my mind. His grip was

a little too tight. His kiss wasn't just eager, it was hungry and possessive. I should have pulled away. I almost did.

We were in the bedroom before I knew it. His hands were on my skin. His mouth was on mine. He was rough, dominant, and completely in control. For a fleeting second I knew this was not my Adam. But I found myself too caught up in the intensity of needing it to be him.

When it was over, I lay in the dark with my mind spinning. Adam was alive. But he wasn't the same. And I couldn't shake the feeling that I didn't really know him at all.

Piper

Adam slept soundly beside me after we made love. I lay there staring at the ceiling. I knew it was crazy that I'd slept with him, but after the heartbreak of thinking he was dead, I couldn't help myself.

The man I loved was alive, and his baby was in my stomach. I'd grieved him, pictured his lifeless body, and now he was here. His chest rose and fell rhythmically. His soft breaths tickled my face. He looked like my love.

But he didn't touch me like him anymore. He didn't talk like him. This wasn't the calm Adam I knew. This new, intense version of him was something else entirely.

I slid out of bed and quietly pulled on a jumper to cover my trembling body. I couldn't be near him. My feet carried me to the kitchen, where I paced the floor clutching a glass of water. I knew whatever Adam had to tell me would change everything, but was I really ready to hear it? Nothing would ever be the same again.

I heard his footsteps before I saw him. When he appeared in the doorway, I stopped pacing and froze. He leaned against the doorframe. His eyes were darker than I'd ever seen them, shadowed and unreadable.

"You're upset," he said simply.

"Upset?" I laughed bitterly, the sound cracking in the quiet room. "I'm beyond upset, Adam. What the hell is going on? You owe me the truth. No more lies. No more games. Just the truth, please." My voice broke, and I hated myself for sounding so desperate.

"Piper, I've been trying to protect you." He sighed, running a hand through his hair as he stepped closer. "I'm the only one who's ever tried to protect you."

"Protect me from what?" I snapped. "You're the one who's been lying to me, sending me notes, making me think I was losing my mind. You let me believe you were dead! How is that protecting me?"

His jaw tightened, and a flash of fear struck my gut.

"From people like Peter! Like your neighbour," he snapped. He ran a hand through his hair and sighed. "It wasn't supposed to be like this."

"Then how was it supposed to be? Just tell me the truth. Who are you?" I shook my head, my frustration boiling over. "Please? I need to know."

He looked at me for a long moment, and for the first time I saw something crack in his facade. His eyes narrowed.

"My name isn't Adam Bell," he said finally. "It never was."

I stared at him, waiting for him to explain, but he looked away. His hands clenched into fists at his sides.

"What are you saying?" I asked, my voice trembling.

He took a step closer and raised his gaze to meet mine.

"The body they found was Adam Bell. The real Adam. I had to become him temporarily, Piper. He had the perfect life for you. So I copied him. I didn't hurt him. Not at first. He was still seeing patients and living his life. I was only pretending. But he was always going to die at some point. His death was symbolic, you see. He had to die to signal me coming into my true self for you. So yes, I killed him. I made sure it was quick. It's not like I had a choice. I needed to be near you."

"What do you mean?" I shook my head, trying to make sense of his words. "Who are you, if not Adam Bell?"

He hesitated, and then the words came tumbling out.

"My name is Caleb."

I had no reaction at first. Then I realised, and the room spun round me. I reached out and gripped the edge of the counter to steady myself as memories flooded my brain.

Not visions.

Memories.

Memories of a little boy. The same boy reflected in the shiny merry-go-round in the hallway photo. The same boy who has haunted me since I was sixteen. The one I haven't seen since the fire.

His face came into full view for the first time in eighteen years.

"No," I whispered, shaking my head. "That's not possible."

"Do you remember me?" he asked as he stepped closer.

I looked up at him. There's a reason I felt so comfortable with Adam so quickly. Not Adam. *Caleb.*

My big brother who I had adored and followed everywhere.

Caleb was the one who protected me from Dad. My real dad. The one with an unfamiliar face but the same eyes and nose. The one Mum locked me in a mental home for when I spoke of remembering him. She wanted to make sure those memories never resurfaced.

"I was there, Piper. I was the boy from your dreams who you've been so desperate to see."

"Oh, Caleb," I gasped. Tears stung my eyes. "I can't believe

217

I forgot you. What happened to you? Why did I forget you?"

"Dad." His whole demeanour changed, and I suddenly felt a chill. "He took it too far, Piper. He was going to kill her or you. I had to stop him. I had to protect you and Mum, but everything went wrong. He died. Mum got scared of me. She thought I was like him, and she made me leave. She kicked me out."

"Caleb, I'm so sorry."

The name felt strange to my tongue. He looked down at the ground, and I fought a sudden urge to reach out to him, not sure how he'd react to my touch.

"I got lost for a bit. And when I found you again, I knew I had to keep you safe no matter what."

"As Adam?"

"As your lover." He raised his gaze to meet my eyes again.

I went from feeling heartbroken to sick to my stomach as I realised the full extent of what had happened between us. I gripped the kitchen counter as the room spun.

"But why, Caleb? Why pretend to be my boyfriend?"

"Because you and I are supposed to be together. Don't you remember our stolen kisses? I'd always make you feel better after Dad left your bedroom."

I sobbed at the memory. Of Dad touching me and making me cry and Caleb making everything better. We didn't know it was so wrong then. We were just kids trying to survive and get what little comfort and affection we could from each other.

"Shh, sweet girl." He reached out to stroke my cheek. "It's okay. I'm here. It's always been us."

"No. This doesn't make any sense." I stumbled back away from his touch, my breath came in sharp, shallow gasps. "I have your *baby* in my womb, Caleb."

"Think about it, Piper. The dreams you've been having, the

things you remember. You know it's all true. This baby is meant to be. We will be a proper family like we always wanted when we were kids."

He stepped closer and laid a hand on my stomach. More memories flashed through my mind at his touch—the fire, the little boy, the way he'd turned to me before disappearing into the flames.

"What about the fire? Was it really my fault?"

"Yes. You started the fire when you couldn't deal with me not being there. You covered the room in oil and lit a match determined to burn the whole fucking neighbourhood down in anger because you loved me so much."

My stomach twisted, bile rising in my throat. I remembered. It was all coming back to me. My love for my brother was too much.

It was *wrong*.

His lips twitched like he wanted to smile.

"We're meant to be, Piper. I've known since we were kids. Remember? We used to play house. You were the wife. I was the husband." His voice dropped to a whisper. "And Dad was the monster."

I pressed a hand to my stomach, bile rising in my throat. I could still feel him on me. His touch, his kiss, his weight. It made my skin crawl.

"I remember. You saved me from the flames," I whispered. "You came from nowhere."

"I was still staying nearby then. Mum kicked me out, but I slept in a treehouse mainly. It was only a few gardens away. I couldn't bear to not be with you. I saw the flames and ran inside to get you. A beam fell on your head a second before I could get to you, but I think your memory loss resulted from being unable to live without me. It was too much trauma to lose me after what Dad did to us."

"But who was the man Mum told me was Dad?"

"Uncle Pete. Dad's twin. He knew what Dad was doing to us and said nothing even though he was always hanging around. Dad always scared the hell out of him when they were kids. I think he'd loved Mum for years. So he stayed with Mum after the fire and looked after you too. They agreed never to tell you about me or Dad. They sent me to a damn mental hospital."

"Why now?" I demanded, my voice shaking. "Why come back now, after all these years?"

"Because I had to," he said simply. "You were all alone without Mum. I needed to get close to you and make sure you were safe. And Adam gave me the opportunity to do that. I borrowed his life because I knew you'd like a guy like him until you remembered about me. He was temporary. That's why I wrote to you explaining I had to kill him. It's time you fell for me again, not him."

I placed my hand on my stomach. The weight of his words pressed down on me like a physical force.

"You killed him," I said. "You killed an innocent stranger for no reason. And Norris Bale?"

"The neighbour? I did what I had to do." He didn't flinch. There wasn't a shred of guilt on his face. "And Norris Bale was a prick. He was always watching the street. I couldn't do anything without him seeing. I had to add cameras in the house to watch you. Obviously I couldn't watch them from my room at Woodview, but a friend helped me to monitor them."

He pointed to something in the corner. A teddy bear on top of a cupboard that I hadn't even noticed in the mess of belongings. He must have put it there when he helped me move in.

"And Peter's gone, too," he announced proudly. "I did that for you. He can't scare you anymore."

Tears spilled down my cheeks as his confession settled over me. My brother. My protector. My stalker.

A serial killer.

I didn't know whether to run as fast as I could or to stay and hug him tight.

"You're insane," I said, my voice trembling as I stared at him. I suddenly remembered how quickly he had reached me the other night and what he said about the police station. "You got to me so quickly because you were already here, and then you knew I'd been waiting outside the police station even though I never mentioned it."

"I did all of this for you. For us."

"Who else have you killed?" I whispered, almost not wanting the answer. "Evelyn? Was that you in the mask?"

"Evelyn was always making you work around those crazy, dangerous men, and I needed to get you back here somehow. Home. With me."

"Did you kill Mum and Uncle Pete?" My heart pounded so loudly I thought it might burst out of my chest.

"No," he growled. "Not on purpose. I wanted Mum alive. I wanted all three of us to be together again. All I had to do was win her trust and show her I'm not an evil psychopath like Dad. But I knew they'd run as soon as they saw me so I asked someone else. That idiot Michael Grey. We were childhood friends stuck at the hospital together, and he owed me. He went crazy when I gave him the gun and started shooting everyone in sight."

The image of Michael Grey from the newspapers flashed through my mind. That definitely hadn't been a picture of

Caleb.

"Why did you get him to do it?"

"I met him at the kids psychiatric institution when Mum sent me away. We were the only two in that hospital who had murdered someone. He'd killed his brother because voices told him too. And we made a pact that we'd kill our parents for each other."

"So what happened to him?"

"After he killed Mum as well as Uncle Peter, he had to die. I convinced him to get a transfer to Woodview. I coached him and told him how to act the whole time he was in the hospital. Then when the time came, I moved into Woodview instead of him. I wanted to be closer to the house when you moved here and it's free food and accommodation. It was pretty easy. I killed him when he was on the way to Woodview. His support worker was someone I already knew from years ago. I gave him a whole load of free coke, he gave me Michael and walked away. No one cared about him or reported him missing."

"And the staff in Woodview just believed you?"

"Yep. They didn't even check my ID when I got there. They pay these staff a pittance and they're mostly good people who assume the best in others. They're easy to fool if you're confident. Who would pretend to be a psychiatric patient, anyway? No one is trying to sneak into these places. You know what I mean. You snuck into the hospital easily."

"I did what I had to," I snapped.

"So did I. I was right near the house. Just like all those years I watched you and Mum. I even mowed the lawn. I've had the spare key for years."

I stared at him, my chest tightening as the edges of the memories I'd buried deep clawed their way to the surface fully.

Flames. Smoke. The little boy who I loved so much because he was the only person in this world who made me feel safe.

"You're sick," I said, my voice cracking. "Do you hear yourself? You're saying you're my brother, and yet you slept with me!"

The words hung in the air. My stomach churned violently, and I pressed my hand to my mouth, trying to hold back the bile rising in my throat as the full weight of the situation hit me.

"I love you, Piper," he whispered. "I always have. That doesn't change just because of what we are."

"What we are?" I choked out. "You're my brother! Do you understand how disgusting this is? How wrong?"

"You don't need to feel guilty, sweet girl. You didn't know we were siblings before we made the baby," he said calmly, as if that made it better. "I didn't tell you earlier because I knew you wouldn't understand straight away. But this connection we have is real. You can feel it too, can't you?"

"No," I snapped, shaking my head violently. "I don't feel anything but disgust. You lied to me and manipulated me. And now I'm pregnant with your child."

I doubled over, the room spinning around me. Caleb reached for me. I slapped his hand away. Hot tears streamed down my face.

"Don't touch me," I hissed. "Don't you dare touch me."

"Piper," he pleaded, but I couldn't listen anymore.

"Get out," I whispered. "Get out of my house."

He didn't move. His eyes searched mine but I didn't back down.

"I said get out!" I screamed, my voice breaking.

"I'm staying," he whispered, stepping closer. "You can

scream, cry, or push me away, but you'll see, Piper. You'll see it's always been us. Run if you think you can. It won't change anything, Piper. I'll always find you."

Piper

"No. Get out," I yelled. Every muscle in my body trembled.

"You think running will help you?" His voice was soft, almost pitiful. "You're not strong enough to raise this baby without me, Piper. You never have been. It's not your fault. It's *his* for damaging you when you were so little and helpless. I'm the only one who's ever been there for you."

He didn't move. He stood steady like my words were nothing more than noise. He didn't even blink. His smile was patient, like I was throwing a tantrum he'd planned for.

"You're upset," he murmured. "I understand. But we always do this, don't we? You run. I follow. It's a game we've played since we were kids."

"I said get out!" I shouted. My voice cracked. Tears streamed down my face, but he only tilted his head. A faint smile tugged at the corner of his mouth.

"You don't really want that, Piper. You'd be truly alone if I left. Look at how happy you were to see me tonight. That's why I had to let you think I was really gone for a moment. That's why Adam had to die. You needed to see how terrible your life would be without me. No one gets you like I do."

"Yes, I do mean it!" I snapped. "I want you gone and out of

my life!"

"I'm not going anywhere," he said. "You need me whether or not you want to admit it. And now with the baby, you need me more than ever."

A fresh wave of nausea crashed over me. My hands instinctively went to my stomach, the horror of it all suffocating me.

"Don't," I hissed. "Don't you dare talk about the baby."

"Our baby," he breathed. There was something almost tender in his eyes. "This is our chance, Piper. A fresh start. A family."

"A family?" I choked out, my voice breaking with disgust. "You're my brother!"

"And you're my sister," he said simply. "That doesn't change how I feel about you or what we have. We can make this work, Piper. You'll see."

I shook my head, tears continuing to fall as I backed toward the door.

"You're sick," I whispered. "You're disgusting. And I will never let you near this baby."

"You don't get to decide that, Piper." He stepped forward, his expression darkening. "This baby is mine too. You can try to push me away, but you're just scared right now. It's a lot to take in. I'm not going anywhere."

The air in the room felt suffocating. His words crushed me. I had to get out. I had to think. If he wouldn't leave, then I needed to. Without another word, I turned and bolted.

"Piper! You can't run from me!"

I didn't stop or look back. I ran into the night with my mind racing. All I knew was that I had to get away from Caleb. I didn't know where I was going or what I was going to do.

But even as I ran, his words followed me. They wrapped

around me like chains I couldn't break. The truth was out now and there was no escaping it. I stopped running and shakily grabbed my cigarettes and lighter from my pocket. I had three slow drags before remembering I was no longer allowed my vice, and I threw the cigarette onto the floor as I screamed and dropped to my knees in tears.

I remembered Caleb. Memory after memory came crashing back. He was right that I'd loved him more than anything. More than I loved Adam. I realised now I loved Adam because he reminded me of Caleb.

There was always an underlying anger inside me directed at Mum, and I finally knew why. She didn't protect us from Dad. I could never understand why she didn't love us enough to protect us. Then she banished the one person who did and my heart shattered.

Caleb always tried his best to protect me. He was only little then, but he comforted me and kissed me better where Dad had hurt me. He made everything okay again. I couldn't cope without him when Mum sent him away. The rage inside me was unstoppable as I set fire to the house to burn everything when she said he was gone. I wanted to die.

Now I could see why Mum sent him away. She couldn't bring herself to send him away before Dad. He was her baby too. She must have loved him. She loved us both, despite her inability to protect us. I understand that more now as an adult.

But after Dad was gone, she'd sent one baby away to protect the other, and I couldn't even imagine how hard that must have been.

Maybe that's why I sometimes felt resentment toward me from her. Especially when I hated her so much for it, even after my memory loss.

Now I knew. Caleb really had Dad's callous streak. And Mum loved me after all. Maybe she pretended not to care that I rarely visited because she thought I was safer in Harrogate. It all made so much more sense.

But Caleb had abused my love for him. Even back then he'd kissed me and touched me. He'd abused me. Manipulated me into doing what he wanted. Brothers are not supposed to touch their little sisters in that way. I knew that now.

And he'd admitted to the murders.

A chill ran through me at the memory of how casual his tone was when he spoke of the people he'd killed. There was nothing there. He showed no emotion about any of them, not even Mum's accidental shooting. He only showed anger towards Michael Grey for not sticking to the plan.

But I hadn't listened to anyone telling me what to do ever. So despite my need for a family and my deep heartache for how my poor brother's life turned out, I realised that what he wanted from me was the one thing I could never give him. Submission. Caleb didn't love me, he wanted to control me.

I forced myself to straighten on shaky legs and lean against a nearby tree, my breath steadying at the sudden resolve in my chest. Caleb was my responsibility. I had spent my whole life waiting to be saved by Adam, by Mum, by anyone who would fight for me. But no one was coming. It had to be me.

Caleb had protected me once. But now he was the monster in the dark, and it was my turn to stop him. And if I couldn't, then I'd make damn sure he'd hurt no one ever again.

Swanson

Swanson stood on the doorstep of Piper's house with his hand hovering over the doorbell. Hart shifted next to him. Her sharp eyes scanned the street. The house was quiet, but Swanson couldn't shake the unease curling in his stomach. After everything Perry Vance had told them, he knew they were running out of time.

He knocked loudly. They waited, exchanging a glance as the seconds stretched. Just as Swanson was about to knock again, the door swung open and a man stepped out to greet them.

"Hi there," the man said, smiling warmly. He was tall, broad-shouldered, with dark, confident eyes. "Can I help you?"

"I'm Detective Inspector Alex Swanson. This is my colleague Rebecca Hart. We're looking for Piper Roberts. Is she in?" Swanson asked cautiously, his sharp gaze narrowing on the man.

"Ah, you just missed her." The man tilted his head slightly, his expression never faltering. "She popped out to pick up a few things. I can tell her you stopped by, though. My name is Caleb."

"Do you know where she went? When will she be back?" Hart crossed her arms as she studied him. His charm had no effect on her. "She hasn't answered her phone."

"Afraid not," he said with an apologetic shrug. "She didn't say, just that she wouldn't be too long."

"When did she leave?" Hart tried again.

"Just a few minutes ago."

Swanson's jaw clenched. Something about Caleb's polished demeanour grated against him. He was too smooth or too calm. He hadn't even asked why they wanted to speak to Piper. Most normal people panicked when unannounced detectives show up on the door asking for loved ones.

"If you could have her call me as soon as possible, I'd appreciate it," Swanson said, handing over his card. "It's important."

"Of course," Caleb replied as he tucked the card into his pocket with a charming smile. Swanson resisted the urge to knock it off his face. "I'll make sure she gets it."

Swanson nodded stiffly, his instincts screaming at him as he turned away. He didn't miss the way Caleb stood in the doorway watching them leave, that faint smile still playing on his lips.

As soon as they were back in the car, Hart glanced at Swanson.

"Well, that wasn't creepy at all," she said.

Swanson grunted, his grip on the steering wheel tightening as he started the car.

"I don't buy it. Something's off about him."

"You think he's lying?"

"I don't know," Swanson said, his jaw tight. "We've got the address for Woodview. Let's see if Michael Grey is really there. If he is, we can arrest him and keep Piper safe that way."

Swanson drove off toward Woodview, which was only a few streets away from Piper's house. The non-secure care home was tucked away in a quiet residential street like most halfway houses across the UK. Inside, the receptionist greeted them with a polite but tired smile.

"We're looking for Michael Grey," Swanson said, flashing his badge. "We understand he lives here."

"Michael Grey... let me check where he is." The receptionist frowned slightly, her fingers tapping at her keyboard.

Swanson's gaze wandered as they waited, landing on a bulletin board mounted on the wall behind the reception desk. It was covered in photos. Patients smiling at Christmas parties, group outings, awards for achievements. The faces stared back at him, some joyful, others reserved. But one thing struck him immediately.

There was no Michael Grey.

"I don't see him anywhere on the board," Swanson said to the receptionist. "Why not?"

"Oh, that's strange," the receptionist replied, turning to look at the board. "He should be on there. We make sure everyone gets included in the photos. Oh, there he is."

"Are you sure?" Swanson asked, his tone sharp as he stepped closer to the board.

"Absolutely." She stood, walking up to the board to point at a photo. "Right here, see? That's Michael."

Swanson's stomach dropped.

It wasn't Michael Grey.

It was Caleb.

He felt his breath catch in his throat as he turned to Hart; the realisation hit him like a freight train.

"That's not Michael Grey," he said. "That's Caleb. The man we just left at Piper's house."

Hart's eyes widened, and she glanced back at the photo.

"What the hell?"

"Are you sure this is Michael Grey?" Swanson turned back to the receptionist.

"Yes, that's him," she said confidently. "He's been here a few months now."

Swanson's mind raced, the pieces falling into place with sickening clarity. Caleb wasn't who he claimed to be. And now Piper was nowhere to be found. Swanson whipped around to face Hart.

"We need to move. Now."

Caleb

The sound of the door closing echoed in my ears long after Piper had stormed out. I paced the living room with my hands running through my hair. My thoughts got tangled sometimes, but she would come back. She always did. She needed me, even if she didn't see it yet.

I'd waited so long for this. I'd planned every detail and every step to bring us here. And now she was slipping through my fingers. It wasn't supposed to be like this. She was supposed to understand and remember what we had. She was supposed to love me the way I love her.

The way she always had when we were younger. When she tried to burn the world just to find me.

I moved to the window and scanned the street for any sign of her. The minutes dragged on. Each one caused the tightening in my chest to get worse. My mind replayed our argument over and over as her words stabbed into me like knives.

You're my brother. You're sick.

I clenched my fists as anger bubbled beneath the surface. I knew she didn't mean it. She was confused. It was my fault. I'd overwhelmed her. She needed time. Once she calmed down, she'd see things clearly.

The sound of the door creaking open snapped me out of my

thoughts. My heart leapt as I turned to see her standing there. Her face was pale but her expression was determined.

"You came back," I said, relief flooding through me. I stepped toward her, but she held up a hand and stopped me in my tracks.

"Stay back, Caleb," she said, her voice trembling. She never trembled like that around me. Dad, yes. But not me.

"Piper, I—"

"No!" she yelled.

Piper had always been fiery, but this wasn't her. She was confused. Lost. Scared. I hated that I'd scared her. That wasn't what tonight was supposed to be.

"What's wrong?" I asked, desperate to hug her and make it better.

"I can't do this, Caleb," she said. "You need help."

I needed help? That's what Mum had said before she carted me off. The words cut into my chest. I shook my head gently, trying to show her how wrong she was.

"No," I whispered. I stepped closer to her shaking body. The same one that was carrying our baby. "You don't mean that. We just need time. You'll see. Everything can be okay. We can be okay."

Her hand rested on her stomach. Her protectiveness against me was a knife twisting in my chest. That was our baby. She couldn't keep looking at me like I was a monster. I wasn't like him.

I wasn't Dad.

"You're not okay, Caleb," she said, her voice cracking. "And I can't pretend. You need help. Please. For me. For the baby."

"Don't say that," I snapped, my voice sharper than I intended. Her eyes widened, and I hated myself for the fear I saw there. I softened my tone. "I'm doing all of this for you and the baby, Piper. Don't you see? Everything I've done has been for you. To protect you."

"You're not protecting me." She shook her head as tears spilled down her cheeks. "You're hurting me."

She didn't mean it. She couldn't.

"You don't understand," I replied softly.

I lunged forward and grabbed both of her scarred wrists, the same scars I loved to stroke while she slept, and snapped the cuffs from my pocket around them.

She screamed and tried to pull away as if she feared me, and I shoved a nearby cloth into her mouth, securing it in place with some tape from my other pocket.

"Shh, it's okay, Piper," I soothed. "I got you."

I lifted her over my shoulder as gently as I could with her kicking and screaming, and carried her upstairs to place her on the bed. Luckily the gag muffled her screams. She tried to jump up, and I pushed her back down on the bed.

"Hey, I got you." I pressed her down onto the soft mattress and whispered into her ear. "Don't panic, Piper. I know what will make you feel better."

I kicked her legs open and planted soft kisses on her neck. It always made her feel better, just like it did after Dad hurt her. I kissed away the tears on her cheeks. I needed her to remember what we had.

But when she finally calmed enough to stop the muffled screams, a knock at the door cut through the feeling that was settling between us.

No. Not now.

My stomach sank. I couldn't let anyone interfere, not when we were so close to understanding each other again. Piper kicked out and began her muffled screaming again.

"Don't you dare," I hissed.

Her eyes locked onto mine, and I saw the defiance burning in them and clamped a hand around her throat to quiet her.

Then I heard the downstairs door get kicked in and a shout. That fucking Alex Swanson was coming. But I was done running. He'd have to die too.

It wasn't long until I heard him running up the stairs and then he appeared at the door. The sight of him standing there with his broad frame taking up all the space sent a surge of anger through me. He shouldn't be anywhere fucking near her. I told her in my letters not to let him in. His sharp eyes scanned the room before locking on to me.

"Piper," he said calmly. "Don't worry. You're going to be okay."

"She knows that!" I spat. "She's with me! I would never hurt her. You're the one who will end up hurting her."

She looked back at me, her expression conflicted. Tears streamed her cheeks. Swanson had made her cry. The rage in me turned palpable. Then she turned to him. Swanson's jaw tightened too, his hands flexing at his sides. He stepped inside the room, his gaze never leaving mine.

"We need to have a talk man to man." His tone was neutral but edged with steel. "Let Piper go."

"This is none of your business," I growled. "She's *my* sister, and she's going nowhere."

Something flickered across his face. Surprise maybe. I wasn't sure. Maybe he didn't know everything like he thought he did. I stepped forward as a warning to him he wasn't getting anywhere near her. He didn't back down. Of course he didn't. Men like him never did.

They thought they were the heroes. But he didn't know Piper like I did. I tried warning her about letting an imposter like him in our space but she didn't understand. He didn't know what we'd survived together. He didn't know her at all.

"It becomes my business when people get hurt," Swanson said. "Let's take a step back and talk this through."

"Talk?" I let out a bitter laugh. "You think you can just walk in here and talk and fix this? You don't understand. Piper and I belong together."

Swanson took another step inside the room. I smirked. Soon he would be right where I wanted him.

"This isn't the way, Caleb. If you care about her, you'll let her go so she can make her own mind up. You'll let us help you."

"You think you're the hero here, don't you?" I snarled, my fists clenching. "You think you can just waltz in and take her away from me? She's mine! She always has been."

I jumped back as another face appeared behind Swanson. It was the hard-faced woman he was with earlier who kept asking me about times. I glared at her.

"Backup's here," she gloated to Swanson. The twisted little bitch. She probably let him bend her over whenever he fucking asked, and he's in here pretending to be Piper's hero.

Then the sirens came blaring from the distance. I could hear at least three police cars heading our way.

"See? It's over. She's not yours," Swanson said evenly. "She's her own person. And right now, she's scared. Look at her, Caleb. Look at what you're doing to her. She's terrified of you."

I glanced at Piper. The fear in her eyes cut deeper than any blade. But beneath it there was something else. Sadness. Pity.

Love?

"No," I muttered, shaking my head. "She doesn't mean it. She's just confused."

But Piper shook her head defiantly. My vision blurred, my chest tightened as the truth clawed its way into my mind. We had to end it to be together. But I couldn't get past that many police officers.

I grabbed the gun from my back pocket before Swanson could move quick enough to stop me. I fired one shot at Piper and then turned the gun on myself. We would be together. Just not in this lifetime.

Pain exploded in my skull, I fell to the floor, my hands sticky with blood. Piper wasn't moving. I blinked and saw Swanson running to her. He was too late. Now, she would always be mine. The darkness pulled me under. The last thing I saw was her face. Beautiful. Mine. Forever.

Piper

The steady beep of the heart monitor was the only sound in the hospital room. I stared at the ceiling. Its pristine whiteness was a reminder of another truly awful day in my past. I pushed the thoughts away; at least I wasn't getting locked up this time.

My stomach ached with a dull, hollow pain, both physical and emotional. I already knew the truth. The baby was gone.

I couldn't cry. Not yet. I'd spent the night replaying Caleb's last moments in my mind. His words lingered in my brain in a way I knew I'd never get rid of. The boy I'd loved as a child, and the man who had controlled my entire life without me even knowing, was gone. No one had confirmed it to me yet, but I knew it was true. I could feel it. It should have felt like freedom. But all I could feel was loss.

A knock at the door pulled me from my thoughts. Alex Swanson stepped in, followed closely by Rebecca Hart. The sympathy in their eyes was almost unbearable. There was a woman behind them who stayed in the corridor. She smiled at me as she turned away. Her stomach was big and round with a growing baby. I swallowed away the lump in my throat as Swanson pulled a chair to my bedside.

"Piper," Swanson said softly. Hart stood near the door with

her arms crossed and a guarded expression. "How are you feeling?"

"I'm alive," I said simply, my voice hoarse. "I guess that's something."

Swanson nodded. His face was unreadable as always.

"We wanted to check in on you. Make sure you're okay."

"You've been through hell." Hart stepped closer, her sharp gaze softening as she spoke.

"Is that why you're here?" I asked. "To remind me I've been through a lot?"

"No." Swanson sighed, running a hand over his beard. "We're here because you deserve to know what happened before it's in the news."

"Deserve to know what?" The room seemed to close in around me as my heart raced.

"About Caleb," Swanson said, his tone gentle. "He's dead, Piper. It's over."

The words hung in the air even though I knew they were coming. I swallowed hard and my hands gripped the blanket tightly. The relief I wanted to feel never came. Instead, there was a strange emptiness and a void that would never be filled.

"Dead," I repeated. The word felt foreign to my tongue.

Hart's gaze softened further, but she didn't speak. They were waiting for me to break down and fall apart. But I didn't. Not yet. Never in front of others. Except Caleb.

"Thank you," I said finally, somehow keeping my voice steady. "For stopping him. For being there to save me."

"If you ever need anything, Piper, you call us. Any time." Swanson nodded curtly.

"I will," I lied.

Hart gave me a small nod before they left, and then the

door clicked shut behind them. The silence that followed was deafening. I stared at the door and willed myself to feel something. But the tears wouldn't come. Not yet. Not until I was sure I was alone.

When they finally did, they came in waves. Each sob racked my body with a force I couldn't control. I cried for the babies I'd never met, for the brother I'd loved and lost, for the mother who really loved me, and for the woman I used to be before Caleb broke me completely.

But as the tears subsided, a strange calm settled over me. I wasn't the same woman I'd been when this began. I'd survived the fire Caleb had tried to set in my life, and I would rebuild as I always had. As I did when I was ten and felt so alone. And again when I was eighteen and my parents locked me away. Then again when my parents died and left me alone in this world. Or so I thought.

Now I would survive Caleb.

I reached for my phone with trembling hands, scrolling through my contacts until I found the number I was looking for—the estate agent I'd seen in the local paper.

"Hi," I said when the agent answered, my voice steadier than I'd expected. "I'd like to schedule a meeting. I'm looking to sell a house that was left to me in a will."

The words felt like a promise, not just to myself, but to the life I was determined to create. I might be broken, but I wasn't defeated. I was Piper Roberts. And I was the only Roberts still standing.

Except for the little boy standing in the corner, watching me with a clear face and angry, dark eyes.

Summer

The police station was busy once more as Summer sat at her desk. There was continuous chatter and occasional ringing phones. A glass of water sat untouched beside her. She was filing away the last of some new case notes, and her mind felt restless. She didn't know if it was pregnancy hormones or something else, but Piper's story haunted her.

Not to mention she could've lost Swanson when Caleb Roberts pulled out that damn gun. The thought caused a shot of nausea.

The door opening pulled her from her thoughts. Swanson stepped in with a thin folder in his hand. His face was as grim as ever, and there was a look in his eyes that she hadn't seen in a while. He dropped the folder onto her desk without a word, the papers spilling slightly.

"What's this?" Summer asked, straightening the papers and glancing at the label.

"Hayley Smith," Swanson said, his tone heavy. "They found her."

Summer froze. She'd almost forgotten about poor Hayley Smith in the aftermath. The woman who had unknowingly stumbled into Caleb Roberts' web of obsession and control.

The same Hayley that Perry Vance had been too terrified to talk about for so long.

"They found her body?" she asked.

Swanson nodded, pulling out a chair and sitting across from her.

"One team searching Caleb's known addresses came across a storage unit he rented under an alias. Her body was inside."

"When?"

"Early this morning," Swanson replied. "He'd locked the unit up tight. No one would've known it was there if we hadn't been looking."

"Do we know how long she's been there?" Summer leaned back in her chair, another wave of nausea rolling through her.

"Too long," Swanson said grimly. "Preliminary reports say it's likely been a couple of weeks. Michael Grey's body was in there too, and we confirmed who the real Adam Bell was. It turned out he was having no end of issues with someone using his identity to get credit cards and a loan. Perry Vance was transferred to a secure psychiatric facility. He'll never be free, but at least he was alive. And there was a third body at the unit of a patient from Pinevale House. Peter."

The image of Hayley's smiling face flashed in her mind, drawn from the photos they'd circulated during the missing person investigation. Poor Hayley had no idea what she'd walked into that day as she made her way to check on Perry Vance on the way home from work.

"This wasn't just about Piper," Summer said softly, more to herself than to Swanson. "He wanted control over everyone around her."

"Power," Swanson agreed, his voice flat. "That's all it ever was for someone like him. He couldn't stand being denied."

Summer closed the folder, her fingers lightly touching the edges of the pages.

"What happens next now that he's dead?" she asked.

"We have to finish the story without him." Swanson leaned back, crossing his arms over his chest. "We need to piece everything together, trace every step Caleb took, every lie he told, every person he hurt. We owe that much to Hayley and Piper. Norris Bale and Perry Vance. To everyone he left behind."

His words settled in the air. They wouldn't bring Hayley back, and it wouldn't undo the damage he'd done. But it was something.

Summer nodded slowly, her thoughts drifting to Piper. She admired the woman's resilience. She'd been tempted to visit Piper with Swanson at the hospital. Just to offer an ear if she needed one. But when they arrived and found out she'd lost the baby, she'd stayed outside the ward. She didn't want to rub her obvious pregnancy in Piper's face. She picked up the folder again, her eyes lingering on Hayley's name printed neatly on the top.

"What's on your mind?" Swanson asked, his voice cutting through her thoughts.

She hesitated, Piper's trauma settling heavily in her chest. Piper's desperation to hold on to her family even when it hurt her had struck a chord. Their stories were so similar, yet ended so differently.

"My brother," she said finally.

"Eddie?" Swanson's tone softened. She nodded.

"Piper's case reminded me how easy it is to lose someone to mental health."

"Call him," Swanson said simply, his voice steady.

Taking a breath, Summer scrolled through her contacts until she found Eddie's name. Her thumb hovered over the call button for a moment before she pressed it. As the phone rang, she glanced at Swanson, who gave her a small nod before standing and walking out of the room to leave her alone with her thoughts. The call connected, and Eddie's familiar voice filled her ears for the first time in two months.

"Hello?"

"Hey, Eddie. It's me." Summer smiled faintly.

Piper's story had ended in tragedy, but Summer refused to let her own story follow the same path. She wouldn't take anything for granted again. Not her family. Not her babies. Not her life.

And as she spoke to her brother, the weight on her chest finally started to lift.

Thank you so much for reading You'll See! If you have a minute to leave a review on Amazon, I would very much appreciate it.

Have you read the other books in the Fractured Minds series? Check them out on Amazon now at https://mybook.to/fracturedminds.

Fancy more mind twisted thrillers? Check out standalone thriller The Holiday Home on Amazon now at https://mybook.to/HolidayHome.

Also by Ashley Beegan

The Holiday Home

The beautiful, old cottage in the Peak District was the perfect place for Simone to take a much-needed break following a horrific attack. Surrounded by nature and peace, she can finally relax.

Until she realises she isn't alone.

Someone is hiding in the woods, and sneaking inside to leave her unwanted surprises. Her therapist, Theo, insists there is nobody else there, other than the gardener, and she just needs to rest. But as she grows closer to Theo, Simone finds out that this particular cabin has some dark secrets.

Secrets that people will **kill** to protect.

Printed in Great Britain
by Amazon

59460997R00148